Triangles

By Nia Rich

Also by Nia Rich

Never Going Back

My Love Is Deeper

F**k Boy

Lovers Remorse

Triangles

Written by: Nia Rich
Copyright © 2017 Nia Rich

All rights reserved.

Cover: Tina Louise
Editor: Venitia Crawford-Fergus

This is a work of fiction. Names, characters, places are either the product of the authors imagination or are used fictitiously and any resemblance to actual persons, living or dead, business establishments, events, or locals, is entirely coincidental.

Triangles

A love triangle is a romantic relationship between three people. Two people love a third person and the third person loves them both.

"Look, don't run away from it because it's different. Open your mind to something new."

Chapter 1

Raelyn

I turned towards my full-length mirror and removed the towel that I had around my wet body. I used it to pat dry my body before applying lotion. I looked over my naked body in the mirror. Brown skin, one tattoo, small hips, flat stomach, and small breasts. I've thought about getting breasts implants a few times in my life, but I've never had the courage to go under the knife. My twin sister would kill me if I showed up with a brand-new pair of breasts one day anyway. We pretty much have the same size everything. She would flip if I made changes to my body. I figure that I can work with what I have. Besides, my ass makes up for what I lack in breast. I like the size of my ass. People used to call an ass my size an apple bottom. It's not Nikki Minaj thick, but it is round. I turned in the mirror to look at my ass and then smiled. "With this ass, I should have been found someone to tap it." I said to my reflection in the mirror.

I'd been single and celibate for a couple of years. My twin sister Riley would make a joke out of it. She liked to say that I had cob webs on my cookie. I always gave her the finger as she was dying of laughter. I would always tell her to hell with her jokes because I was doing me. I didn't fall in love easy and I trusted seldom, so it was hard for me to let someone into my heart. I don't think I'd ever been in a real relationship. I dated this guy for a while, but I wasn't that into him, and then he decided to get into a relationship that I found out about on social media. I wasn't tripping. I just decided to take a break from men and focus on myself. My vibrators and porn had been satisfying me just fine. I never had to do background checks on them, or sifter through the bullshit to find out if they were worth my time or not. They didn't come with games, lies, kids and baby's mama's either. I could get mine and carry on with my life without a worry in the world.

"Yea but there ain't nothing like a man to scratch that itch for you Raelyn." Riley would say.

Riley is the older of us two. She was born first, a couple of minutes before me. That makes her a bit protective of me. We were supposed to be triplets, but my mom miscarried one while she was pregnant with us. I love that my twin sister is my best friend, but I always hate when Riley would get on me about my sex life. She was always complaining about not having a man, I, on the other hand, didn't want one.

"I have toys to satisfy me. Haven't you ever heard of the rabbit? It will change your life. You will never need a man again." I told her.

She laughed until her stomach hurt and then she said, "I don't know anything about a rabbit, and I don't want to know anything about it."

"I am going to buy you one sister. You will love me for it later." I said.

I was just fine with my single lifestyle and my relationship with my toys, but when I met Laron, everything changed. He wasn't really my type. I like my men simple and clean cut with church boy kind of swag, but he was more like dope boy fresh. He was wearing all black designer label jeans, polo style shirt, construction boots, a gold chain, gold watch, and a gold pinky ring. It wasn't a bad look, but it was the diamond encrusted gold grill he had on his bottom teeth that I wasn't feeling. Although I wasn't interested, his sex appeal caught my attention. I met him while at the club the night of our brother's birthday party. Our older brother Ezekiel, Eazy for short, is an events planner and host for all the major night clubs. That night, Eazy hosted his birthday party at the club my sister and I bartend at. Our boss is cool and let us have that night off so that we could celebrate with our brother. My brother's birthday falls in the middle of summer. Riley and I love it because we have a reason to be extremely under dressed and out and about.

We were chilling in our brother's VIP section with a couple of our closest friends when we decided to circle the nightclub to see who was in there. We circled the first and second floor of the night club. We stopped walking several times to give hugs to a bunch of people that we knew. We were heading back to the VIP area when we ran into my sister's ex Jamir. My first instinct was to follow our friends Taji and Cherry to the bar, but I stayed and chatted. Next thing I knew, he was signaling for his friend to come over there to meet me. I saw a tall, light skinned guy with dreads making his way through the crowd towards us. At first sight, I wasn't feeling his look, but he had a sex appeal and some swag that caught my attention. He leaned in to ask me my name and I caught a whiff of the cologne he had on. His scent was sexy, and his movements were slow and confident. I felt tingles throughout my body when I heard his deep voice. He told me that his name was Laron. I took a quick overview of his whole look before I told him my name. He smiled and asked me if I would like a drink. That is when I saw that damn gold grill on his bottom teeth. I thought, *"Uuugh"*

I turned down the drink because I already had enough. We stood there and talked for a couple of minutes before Cherry and Taji made it back to us, and then the rest of Jamir's friends came over by us. I was glad because I could focus my attention on everyone else and not the thumping going on in my panties. I told myself that it wasn't Laron that had that effect on me because he wasn't my type. I blamed it on the alcohol. It most definitely had to be the alcohol.

All eight of us hung out for a while at the club, and then we all left the club to go to the pizza spot across the street. Me, my sister, and our friends Cherry and Taji sat there for a while eating our pizza slices, talking, and laughing with Jamir and his four friends. After a few jokes and laughs, Laron asked, "So what are you all doing after this?"

His deep voice added to his sex appeal for sure. I heard it over the loud music in the club, but it *really* caught my attention sitting at the table. I felt tingles through my body again. *"Does this dude really have me feeling this way?"* I asked myself. I didn't want him to notice that I was feeling him, so I decided to hit him with a joke.

"Don't tell me your one of those Netflix and chill types." I said with a smile. Everyone at the table laughed. I wiped my hands on a napkin.

Laron said, "Nah, I was trying to see if y'all wanted to hit a little after set at my boy's house. It's not ratchet. He plays for the Timberwolves."

I wiped my hands on the napkin I had in front of me. I looked at Riley. We have a way of communicating without speaking. The look she gave me told me that she didn't want to go.

I said, "No that's ok. We are going to get out of here, maybe next time."

In my opinion, after parties are always ratchet; just on various levels. Riley feels the same way. The four of us ladies stood up, grabbed our empty paper plates, and said our goodbyes to the guys. We walked over to the trash bins to throw our things away. All the guys stood up one by one to leave too. I saw Jamir approach Riley, and then Laron walked up to me.

"Hey, Ms. lady, your name was Raelyn, right?

"Yes."

"Can I get your number, so I can call you sometime?" he asked. He already had his phone in hand.

My mind said, *"No,"* but my mouth said, "Sure."

Honestly, I was hoping that he wouldn't ask, so I could have a reason to blame the whole experience on the alcohol. I'm not sure why I agreed to take his number. Most times, I curve dude's quick, but not Laron. He unwantedly had my attention. Laron handed me his phone after unlocking it. I dialed my number, clicked on add contact, typed my name in, and hit save. I handed him his phone back. Laron took it and tapped the screen to dial my number. My phone started buzzing in my clutch purse. I pulled my phone out and showed Laron the screen. When he saw his number flashing across the screen he nodded his head and said, "Ok I'll hit you up Ms. Raelyn."

Me, Riley, and our friends, left the pizza restaurant and started walking back to the parking ramp where our cars were parked. I was thinking that maybe my sister was right. Maybe it was time to dust off my flower and let it bloom again, and then I jumped back to reality. *Hell no, dudes lie, and men ain't shit. If all men could be more like my father, I wouldn't mind. I am better off loving myself. I can't wait to get home to my rabbit.* I thought, and then Riley broke my thoughts.

"You like him, don't you?" She asked as we were walking down the street. We were approaching the corner of Hennepin Avenue and 4th Street where the Gay 90's nightclub is. There were a few transgender females standing on the corner smoking a cigarette. Once we made it to the corner we could see a few Drag Queens standing in the patio section outside of the nightclub talking and laughing. There was a bachelorette party of women standing outside in the patio section wearing sashes, tiara's and penis necklaces. All four of us looked over there and smiled, and then I answered Riley's question.

"I don't know. He's not really my type." I said as we waited for the stop light to turn green, so we could cross the street.

"Don't lie. I know you do because you wouldn't have given him your number if you didn't." Riley said.

"He was fine!" Our friend Taji said.

"He was alright." I said.

The light turned green and we started walking across the street. A couple of cute guys spoke to us when they walked past us going in the opposite direction. Taji and Cherry flirted a little with the guys and then they turned their attention back to me and Riley.

"His dreads were nice sis." Riley said about Laron.

"I love a man with nice lips." Taji said.

"And those eyes though!" our friend Cherry chimed in.

"Ok girl!" Taji said as she slapped hands with Cherry.

"Y'all know I like my men to be chocolate."

"Girl please that peanut butter skin and those salmon colored lips." Cherry said.

"Ha! They *were* salmon colored!" Riley said while laughing.

"What the hell? Who uses salmon as a color reference?" I asked.

"It's a real color. Look it up." she said.

"We sound hungry talking about peanut butter, chocolate, and salmon." I said and laughed. Everyone else laughed with me.

"So, are you gonna let him, do you?" Cherry asked.

"What? What kind of question is that? I am not thinking about that." I said.

The truth is, I *was* thinking about that. I didn't stop thinking about *that* the whole ride home. The patron shots had me on one, and I could not get Laron off my mind, so when I got home, I let my toy become Laron, and he gave me pleasure all night long until I decided to go to sleep.

Chapter 2

Raelyn

I woke up the next morning still feeling a little buzzed from the patron shots. I slid out of bed and stumbled to the bathroom to wash my face and brush my teeth. Laron was on my mind. I felt like I needed vibrator addiction counseling judging by the amount of times I pleasured myself while fantasizing about him the night before. After I was finished washing up, I decided to let Laron, the toy, give me some morning pleasure. I opened my bedroom drawer and pulled out my favorite pink toy. I laid back in my bed and closed my eyes. I thought about how sexy Laron was to me the night before. I imagined him taking my nipples into his mouth, kissing me down my body, past my belly button, and putting his lips on my clit. I moaned and felt myself about to reach my orgasm. I moaned and used my free hand to grip my sheets. I had my vibrator on the right spot. I moaned his name. *"Laron."* I could feel it. My orgasm was right there, and then my phone started ringing. I tried to ignore it, but the sound broke my vibe and all I could hear was my phone playing that damn Chris Brown song I had as my ring tone. "Uuugh" I said out loud. I turned my vibrator off and laid it on the bed beside me. *Next time, I will remember to make sure that my ringer is off when I am trying to get mine.* I thought. I reached over to my nightstand to get my phone so that I could check my missed call. It was an unsaved number. When I searched through my call log, I realized that it was the number Laron called me from the night before.

"Oh, my gosh." I said. He *would* call right when I was in the middle of fantasizing about him. I was not sure why I felt a little embarrassed. It wasn't like he knew what I was doing. I went back and forth in my head for a couple of minutes about whether I wanted to call him back. I really could've gone back to getting mine, and then return the call later. Without any further thought, I tapped the screen on the missed call. *I might as well try something new. Hell, if*

his conversation is whack I can just never call him again. I thought.

Laron answered after a couple of rings.

"Hello?"

"Um, Hi, is this Laron?"

"Yes, Raelyn, right?"

"Yes."

"How are you doing?" My body tingled again at the sound of his deep voice.

"I am doing fine. How are you?"

"I'm good. I hope I didn't disturb you."

"Uh no, not really." I giggled a little thinking about what I was doing when he called. "What are you doing up so early?" I asked.

He chuckled. "I had some things to take care of for work."

"Oh ok."

My phone beeped. I pulled the phone away from my ear to see who was calling. It was Riley.

I said, "Um could you hold for a minute?"

"Yea."

I swiped the screen to answer the incoming call.

"Yo." I said.

"Yo. are you ready to go to the gym?" Riley said.

"Give me about fifteen minutes to get dressed." I responded.

"Alright, text me when you're leaving."

"Alright."

I switched back over to Laron's line.

"Hello."

"Yes."

"Sorry about that."

"It's alright. So, um I had a nice time with you and your friends last night. I was feeling your vibe though. I would love to see you again. Can I take you out to dinner sometime?"

"Sure, that would be great."

"Ok, well I know you are a bartender so how does your schedule work?"

"Well I work weekends"

"Alright, so your Monday through Wednesdays are free?"

"Yes."

"Ok, so how about this Monday?"

"That sounds great." I responded.

"Alright Ms. Lady, I'll hit you up."

"Alright. Bye."

I hadn't been on a date in so long, I felt kind of excited about it. After the phone hung up, I danced around my apartment as I logged on to my social networking page. I looked at the pictures Eazy and Riley tagged me in from the party the night before. I smiled and pressed the like button on all of them. I went to my kitchen to make myself a protein shake. With my protein shake in hand, I walked back to my living room and put the cup on the coffee table, and then I went into my bathroom to take a quick shower. After the quick shower, I threw on my workout clothes, grabbed my cup, phone, and keys and left out of the door.

***

Riley was waiting in her car in the parking lot for me as usual. She is always early, and I am always on time. I parked in an empty spot a few cars away from Riley's. It was the only spot available. Riley saw me park and got out of her car to meet me, so we could walk together into the gym.

"Your late Rae" she said.

"I know Ri, and you're mad." I said.

"Yes."

"You'll get over it."

Riley smacked me on my butt hard.

"Ow. Ok. I am sorry." I said.

"You better be. You're never late. You're looking kind of like Taji right now."

I started laughing. "Where is she anyway? She must not be coming today."

"No, I guess her, and her man got into it or something and she is not in the mood."

"Um hum. They are always arguing."

"I know. Anyways, let's go so I can kill you on this treadmill."

I said. "We'll see who'll be dying and it sure is not going to be me."

Riley smiled and rolled her eyes "Ok."

We walked into the gym and went straight to the treadmill. Riley was right. I almost died on the treadmill ten minutes into the workout. I blamed it on the alcohol from the night before.

"I am not trying to hear that." Riley said as we wiped down the treadmill machines with Clorox cleaner wipes. We'd just finished thirty minutes of intense cardio, and we were heading to the weight machines. We walked over to one of the machines that works out the arms. I walked over to the side of the machine to adjust the weight for us. Riley sat down first to do a few sets.

"That party was lit last night." she said.

"Yes, Eazy always has a lit party especially for his birthday." I said.

"His friends were getting on my nerves." she said.

"Always." I laughed.

"What was up with the one that kept offering to buy us drinks after we told him that we were cool. I was ready to smack his drunk ass." Riley said.

I laughed and said, "Eazy was looking like he was going to beat him down."

"Yea, you know big bro does not play that."

That guy from last night called me this morning." I said while watching Riley do her sets.

"What!? Which one? The chocolate cutie from VIP? He was fine." Riley said.

"I know but it wasn't him. The other one called." I said.

"The one that was with my ex?"

"Yes. Do you know him?"

"No. I have never seen him before, so he must be a new friend of Jamir's. He is fine too."

After Riley did a few sets, she stood up. I sat down, grabbed the handles, and pulled them towards my stomach.

I said. "Girl every time he talks to me my body tingles."

"Haha. He got that magic. So, *you do* like him?" Riley laughed.

"I don't know but he certainly has sex appeal." I said while smiling.

"He must have really been interested or thirsty as hell to be calling you the next morning sister." Riley said with her hand on her hip. She was standing on the side of the machine watching me do my sets.

"I know that's what I was thinking." I said. I exhaled loudly. The muscles in my arms were starting to burn.

"He seems like kind of a bad boy type though." I said.

"I know. Just the kind I like." Riley smiled.

"That's your problem. You know I like good, church raised, mama's boys."

"That's your problem. You're sitting around waiting on your knight and shining armor when you should be letting one of these bad boys tap that, smack that, flip that, and rub it down."

I laughed and said, "Sister where did you get that old school saying?"

"From our older cousin, but seriously it still works for what we're talking about." she said and laughed.

"He asked to take me out to dinner, and get this, he is going to choose where he wants to take me. Who does that these days?"

"Nobody under thirty."

I stood up. We walked over to the next machine. Riley set the weight and then she sat down. She reached up to grab the handles and then she pulled the handles down towards her chest.

"I am kind of excited to see how this date turns out." she said.

"Me too."

Riley did a couple of sets and then she stood up. I sat down and reached up to grab the handles and pulled them down to my chest.

I asked. "So, what's up with Jamir?"

Jamir broke my sister's heart. I was surprised to see her talking to him. I secretly hoped that she wasn't going to go that route again. Jamir was a couple of years older than her and he played a lot of games. I didn't want to see her hurt like the first time.

"I was shocked to see him out." she said.

"I was too. I thought he was married." I said.

"Well that was the last I heard." Riley said. She winced as she pulled the bar down to her chest for the last time. Riley released the handles slowly and then she stood up. We both started walking towards the mats and fitness balls.

"He was looking good though." she said.

"He was girl." I said. I wanted to say more, but I kept my opinion to myself.

We sat down to start stretching.

Riley said. "But I am not messing with a married man."

I said, "Absolutely not."

Chapter 3

Raelyn

I turned and looked at myself in my full-length mirror. Short, black, loose fitting, long sleeve dress with slits down the sleeves, turquoise 4-inch heels, and silver earrings. Weave slayed and laid. I was feeling good. I checked my cell phone to check the time. It was forty-five minutes after six, and I had fifteen minutes to get to where I was supposed to be meeting Laron for our date. Luckily, I only live a few minutes from our meeting spot. I put on some clear lip gloss and looked over my make-up. I sprayed on some Beyoncé perfume since I was feeling like the singer with my new weave.

I grabbed my turquoise snake skin clutch and headed out of the door. I pulled out of the underground garage, drove past Dunn Brothers, and took a right turn on Hennepin Avenue. I drove past the college, a bunch of restaurants, bars, and theaters. I stopped at the stop light on 7th Street and Hennepin Avenue. I watched a few couples cross the street and then I took a left. Halfway down the block I turned into the parking ramp on the right. I drove downwards to the first level. After getting a ticket for parking I pulled in and parked in an available space. I took my phone out of my clutch and text messaged Laron to let him know that I had made it. I got out of the car and took the elevator up to a level that lead me outside. Once outside, I stood near the corner to wait for Laron. He walked up from behind me. He tapped me on the shoulder. I turned around, smiled, and hugged him. That tingle I felt before, hit me again. He smelled so good. His hug was warm, and he squeezed me like he missed me.

"Hey Beautiful." Laron said while handing me a single red rose.

"Hi and thank you." I took the rose and smiled. I put the rose to my nose to smell it.

"You look gorgeous." he said.

"Thank you. You look good." I said still smiling.

Laron didn't look bad. He looked more polished than he did the night we met. He wasn't wearing his diamond grill on his bottom teeth, and he had his dreads twisted up into a nice style. He was wearing slacks, and a long sleeve button up with the sleeves rolled up and two buttons opened at the top. He had on a nice pair of dress shoes. He didn't have any of the gaudy jewelry he was wearing at the club. *This is more like it. He cleans up well.* I thought.

We walked arm and arm across the street to the restaurant on the corner. We walked in and took the stairs up to the roof. There were a bunch of candle lit tables lining the edge of the roof. The railings lining the roof prevent you from falling over, and the tables gave a beautiful view of the city. A fireplace was in the middle of the roof area lit up the roof giving it a romantic feel. We chose one of the tables that was near the railings, so we could look out over the city. He pulled my chair out for me. I sat down. He smiled at me and sat down. When the waitress arrived, we ordered wine and some appetizers.

"Your hair looks really nice." he said to start the conversation.

"Thank you. Who twists your locks?" I responded.

"This little shop on the Northside." he said.

"They do a decent job." I said.

"Thank you. How was your day?"

"It was peaceful."

"Do you do anything on your days off?"

"Not really. I work out and run errands."

"Do you enjoy bartending?"

"I do."

"How long have you been doing it?"

"A few years."

He smiled. I smiled. He was so sexy to me. I was having a tough time focusing and not getting googly eyed. Only God and Laron would know if I accomplished that.

"What do you do?" I asked.

"I am a photographer. I work for two major black magazines. I do their photoshoots for their spreads.

I smiled and nodded my head and said, "Impressive. So, that means you work with celebrities."

"Sometimes. Mostly models."

"That is exciting." I said.

"It's not all what it's cracked up to be trust me. Plus, it keeps me busy and in and out of town a lot."

The waitress came back to take our orders. After we ordered food we spent some more time getting to know each other.

"Do you have children?" he asked.

I responded, "No. how about you?"

"No. Not yet at least."

"I take it that you want kids someday."

"Absolutely."

The waitress brought our food to the table. We ate, laughed, and talked. I couldn't tell you much about what we talked about because I was too busy checking him out. He was looking too sexy, and after a couple of glasses of wine, the only thing I could think about was what sex would be like with him. My mind got caught up in the thought of him inside of me in every position, stretching my walls out to his size, and the sweet nectar of my wet peach making him go deeper and deeper into me-

"Raelyn." That brought out of my fantasy and back into the conversation.

"Huh?" I smiled and rubbed my long tresses.

"Where were you? Seemed like I lost you for a moment."

"I was here." I lied. Me and my mind were deep in the gutter.

"I hope so. I hope that I am not boring you."

"No not at all."

Laron smiled showing off his bright whites. I smiled back. *Raelyn girl get it together.* I thought. My mind kept drifting back into the gutter. I couldn't keep my mind out of his pants. By the look in his eyes, I could tell that his mind was in my panties. When dinner was over we walked arm and arm back to the parking garage where I was parked. We stood on the side of my car by the driver's door.

"I like you Ms. Raelyn."

"I like you too Laron."

He leaned in to kiss me and I didn't resist his pink lips. Our kiss got a little steamy when he slipped me his tongue. I tasted his tongue and gave him mine. He pressed his body up against mine and we sort of leaned back onto my car. I felt my peach start to get wet. I felt him slide his hand up my dress and palm my ass. Normally, I would have stopped and smacked the shit out of him, but I was off a bottle of wine, and caught up in his rapture. He could have touched me anywhere the way I was feeling.

"I wanna taste you." he said while kissing me. I felt that tingly sensation through my body again.

"Right now?" I asked.

"Right now." Laron said. He stopped kissing me and looked me in my eyes.

"Where?" I asked.

"In your car." he said.

I thought about getting into the back seat of my car, but I knew there had to be cameras somewhere in the parking ramp. The sound of people coming interrupted our moment. Laron stepped back.

"I'm sorry. I didn't mean to be so forward." he said.

"I want to." I said as I stepped towards him.

"For real?"

"Yes." I responded with a devilish grin

"We can go to my truck, I have dark tints on the windows."

"Ok."

I never did stuff like that, but there was something exciting about the spontaneity of the moment. Getting my box eaten, in a dingy parking garage, by a sexy man, in the backseat of his car was all wrong, but it felt right. I wasn't thinking. Maybe it was the liquor, or maybe it was just him, but in that moment, I was just feeling wild and impulsive, and pretty much down for whatever. I followed him to his truck. It was parked up against the wall a few cars down from mine. I got into the backseat first and he followed. Laron didn't waste any time pulling my panties down after he shut the door. As soon as his soft lips kissed my box I melted. The two-year long hiatus from a man's touch had me purring like a kitten. He rubbed his tongue across my pearl in a slow motion as he tongue kissed my lower lips the same way he had kissed my lips a few minutes prior.

"Mmmm" I moaned as I felt his lips and tongue go work on my box.

Laron spread my lips with two of his fingers and began flicking his tongue in a fast motion on my pearl, and then he sucked on it. I closed my eyes and leaned my head back. For that moment, I was no longer in the parking garage in the back seat of his truck; I was on a bed of rose petals. I didn't care about the possible cameras in the garage, or people coming. The only thing on my mind was the O that I was about to get. I put one of my hands into his dreads. My O was coming, and it felt better than the orgasm I get every day from my vibrators.

"Ah yes!" I squeezed my eyes shut and gripped his dreads as my orgasm rocked my whole body. "Oh, my gawwd." I moaned.

I was frozen after my body jerked a couple of times. I felt like I almost blacked out. When my body relaxed, and I regained consciousness, Laron backed up and smiled at me. I smiled back at him as I sat up and pulled my panties back up. He wiped his mouth with his hand and then kissed me. He opened the car door and got out. I followed him out and he walked me back to my car like nothing happened.

"I had a wonderful time with you Ms. Raelyn. I hope that we can do it again soon." he said with a smile and a look of satisfaction on his face.

"Me too. Thank you." I said. He opened my car door for me and waited for me to get inside. I started my car and then he walked back to his.

I couldn't wait to call Riley and tell her about the date. I was buzzing all over with excitement about Laron. The date went *way* better than I expected. *Way Better.* I picked up my phone and spoke into the voice dialer. "Dial Riley." I said into the phone. The phone located Riley's number and dialed it. She picked up after the third ring.

"Yo!" Riley said.

"Yo! Took you long enough to answer." I said.

"Sorry I was in the middle of doing a homework assignment."

"Oh."

"So how did it go!?" Riley asked excitedly.

"Oh my God sis it felt like a fairytale." I said in a soft dreamy voice.

"Really?!"

"Yes"

"We had a candle light dinner on the roof top, he pulled my chair out for me. His conversation was good. He even gave me a rose."

"Oh wow. That is almost too perfect."

"It felt too good to be true. Nobody is this perfect."

"Well you know what they say girl. When it feels like it's too good to be true; it probably is."

"Shut up Riley."

Riley started laughing and said, "I am just saying."

I laughed too. "Look I am not going to let you kill my vibe." I started singing, "Bitch don't kill my vibe, Bitch don't kill my vibe," into the phone.

Riley laughed again and said, "Anyways I am glad that you finally got out and had an enjoyable time with a man. It is about time that you get some male attention."

"Maybe a little too much male attention."

"What you mean?"

"He ate the cookie." I said bashfully.

"WHAT!"

"Yes." I laughed.

"When? How!?"

"In the parking garage in the back seat of his truck."

"Girl, stop! That is ratchet! I can't believe you sister! Ms. I'm An Angel actually did something like that!?"

"It was actually hella sexy and fun."

"Oh my God. So, is he a keeper?"

"Well, we shall see." I said.

"He better be. He's eating cookies in the backseat of trucks and stuff."

I laughed and then I said, "I'll let you get back to your homework."

"Wait. Before you go, guess who I have been spending some time with?"

"Who?"

"Jamir."

Chapter 4

Riley

Riley met Jamir a few years ago, while working at the club with Raelyn. He was a mechanic and well-known drug dealer. He broke it off with Riley with no explanation. He just stopped calling one day. A couple of years later, Riley heard through the grapevine that he had gotten married. She was angry when he broke up with her, but she moved on and put her focus on work and school. She'd been trying to finish college, so she could get out of the bartending business. Riley was burnt out on bartending and was ready to get a new career started. It would make their parents happy. They never liked that Riley and Raelyn worked at the club. They always wanted them to focus on their education, so they could have thriving careers. Riley was determined to make her parents happy. Raelyn, on the other hand, was comfortable working at the club and planned to stay there.

After Jamir broke up with Riley, she would still think of him from time to time. She wondered why he broke it off with her so abruptly. She figured that the girl he married had something to do with it. Riley tried to date a couple of guys, but it went nowhere. One of the guys she had been dating wanted more than a casual dating situation, but she wouldn't give him a chance. He was too much of a good guy and he didn't have the bad boy swag that Jamir had. When she ran into Jamir in the club that night, her feelings for him resurfaced. Riley never got over Jamir completely, so it was easy for her to pick back up where they left off.

After talking to Jamir over the phone and having lunch a couple of times, Raelyn invited Jamir over to her place for dinner. She had spent hours trying to get things together for a perfect dinner. Riley finished getting dressed, and then she walked into the kitchen to check on the food she had cooking. Riley opened the oven to check on the lasagna. Judging by the way the cheese was browning on the top the lasagna, she knew that it was done. She turned the oven off and used an oven mitt to pull the glass pan out of the oven. Riley set the pan on the stove to cool off. She reached in the refrigerator to take out the salad that she'd prepared earlier and set it on the dining room table. Riley doesn't enjoy cooking, but she can do a little something, something.

The doorbell rang to her second-floor duplex apartment. Riley headed towards the door. She stopped at the full-length mirror on her wall next to the door before going to answer it. The gold eye shadow she had on her eye lids was popping, and her black t-shirt dress was fitting like a glove. Riley readjusted her tight dress, fluffed her kinky curly hair weave, and rubbed her maroon colored lips together. She walked down the wood stairs to open the door for Jamir. The stairs crackled a little underneath her bare feet. She was so excited that she forgot to put on her house slippers. When Riley reached the bottom of the steps, she opened the heavy wood door and then she opened the screen door. Jamir stepped in and hugged Riley. She damn near leaped into his arms and kissed him. Jamir picked Riley up while hugging her causing her t-shirt dress to lift. Riley reached back to pull her dress down to cover her butt cheeks. Jamir laughed, put her down, and patted her on her backside.

"Look at you soul sista. You smell good." he said speaking of her afro-centric look, and the sweet-smelling oil that Riley was wearing.

"Thank you." Riley said flirtatiously.

After she closed and locked both doors, Jamir followed Riley back up the wood stairs to her apartment. Jamir walked into her candle lit apartment and sat down on her couch. The aroma therapy scent from the candles permeated the apartment. Her television was set on one of the Music Choice channels playing RnB music.

"This is nice Riley." Jamir said.

Riley smiled and thanked him again. She told him to have a seat at the table and then she walked into the kitchen to grab a bottle of wine out of the refrigerator. Jamir stood up and walked over to her table to sit down. Riley put the bottle of red wine on the dining room table, smiled at Jamir again, and then she turned to walk back into the kitchen to get the food. Jamir watched her backside jiggle in the t-shirt dress she was wearing. He smiled, stood up, and walked into the kitchen.

"Do you need some help?" he asked Riley.

He stood behind her placing his midsection right on her backside. He gently rubbed his hands from her shoulders down to her arms and kissed her shoulder. Riley felt his lips on her shoulder and smiled. She wanted him and was trying her best control her desires.

Riley said, "Um, would you mind carrying this pot over to the table?"

"I don't mind." he said.

She handed him the oven mitts. Jamir picked up the warm pan and carried it to the table. Riley followed him with a plate of warm garlic bread. They sat down at the table. Jamir popped the cork out of the bottle of red wine and poured wine into both of their glasses. Riley put lasagna, salad, and garlic bread on their plates. She led them in prayer and then they began to eat and sip on their wine.

They ate in silence for a moment and then Riley said, "I never asked what you do now."

"I am still working on cars. I don't know if you remember that I was working towards taking over my uncle's shop."

"Yea because he was sick, right?"

"Yup. Well, he is doing well now, so I am managing his shop for right now."

"That's wonderful."

"Yea. It's doing well. I am going to buy it soon though. He is getting old and still wants me to take over, so he can retire." he said.

"That's amazing."

"Yea well it keeps me out the streets. I got caught up about a year ago, and was almost about to do some time, but I got off. That changed my life. I promised myself and my uncle that I would stay on the straight and narrow, and I don't want to let neither one of us down."

"That's great Jamir." Riley smiled.

"Thanks, so what have you been up to? Are you still bartending?"

Riley put her wine glass down and said, "Yes I am still bartending, but I am in school. I am done with the bartending thing." She took a bite of food.

"I thought you liked bartending?"

"I did, but it's not a career for me. I want a career and an income that is more stable."

"That's what's up. You look really good by the way boo."

"You think so?" she said bashfully.

"Yes. You know you look good." he said smiling at her.

Riley knew. She spent an hour getting ready for his arrival, but she would never tell him that.

Riley thanked him and then she asked, "I've been wanting to ask you something."

"What?"

"What happened to your marriage?"

Jamir sipped the wine and sat the glass down.

"It didn't work out." he said and then he took another bite of food.

Riley asked, "Meaning divorce?"

"Yes." he said.

Riley said, "Oh, I'm sorry." Riley only said that to be nice. She really didn't care. She was happy he got a divorce.

"Yea it's cool. Shit happens you know? Me being in the streets put a strain on my marriage, and then when I caught that case, it just put the nail in the coffin for us."

"That sucks." Riley said. It was another feigned attempt at caring about his marriage ending.

He took another gulp of his wine and looked at Riley. His bedroom eyes were calling

her.

"Come here." Jamir said. He reached out and grabbed her hand from across the table. He pulled her to him. He sat her on his lap, kissed her, and said, "I should have married you."

Jamir had said the magic words. She'd wanted to hear him say that years before when they were dating. Way before his marriage and divorce. Riley had always felt that Jamir was the one for her, she used to pray that he felt the same.

Riley stood up, grabbed Jamir's hand, and pulled him to her bedroom. Jamir sat down on the edge of the bed. Riley stepped back and pulled her dress up over her head. Jamir looked over her smooth brown skin, tight body, large tribal hip tattoo, and her black, lace, panties and bra set. Jamir took off his black t-shirt, so she could see his muscular, dark chocolate, upper body covered in tattoos. Jamir didn't waste another minute after taking off his shirt. He stood up and picked her up and set her on her dresser. Jamir began sucking on her neck as he slipped one of his fingers inside of her. When he heard Riley began to moan, he slid her panties off, kneeled, and began to tongue kiss her bald peach. She watched his goatee get lost in between her legs as he slurped on her juices tasting every sweet drop. His head game hadn't changed a bit. He always knew how to make her legs shake. Riley rubbed his fade haircut a few times as he ate her cookie. He slid his hands underneath her hips and pulled her to him like he was drinking milk out of a bowl. She grinded her hips onto his lips as he sucked on her pearl.

"You taste good baby." he said in between licks.

"Mmmm. Eat that." Riley moaned out loud.

Jamir hit the right spot and she began to squirt. He continued to lick and taste her juices as they drenched his mouth and lips. After Riley's body stopped shuddering from the O he gave her, he stood up. He kissed her and let her taste her juices off his tongue and lips. He then picked Riley up and carried her to the bed. Jamir laid Riley on the bed, got fully undressed, and then he stood over her with his erection in hand. Riley unbuttoned and removed her bra, and then she put his erection into her mouth. Riley forgot how big Jamir was. She could only fit half of him into her mouth. Riley used a lot of saliva while slurping and sucking on him, but she still couldn't get all of him in her mouth. Jamir put his hand on her head and pushed himself further into her mouth which caused her to choke a little. Jamir smiled, pulled his manhood out of her mouth, and picked up the gold packaged condom from her nightstand. He rolled it on and told her to lay down. Jamir slid all his girth into her slowly stretching her walls to his size. Riley dug her nails into his back. She had forgotten what it felt like to have his big tool inside of her. Riley made sounds and grinded her hips back onto him while he sucked one of her nipples.

"Can you handle this?" he asked once he was all the way inside of her.

"Yes" she moaned.

"Are you sure."

"Yes."

"You want it?" Jamir asked.

"Um hum." Riley moaned.

Jamir took one of her legs, placed it onto his shoulder, and dug deep inside of her.

"Ahh Jamir!" Riley yelped when she felt the pain and pleasure of him stretching her walls and hitting her spot at the same time. As he pumped in and out of her, Riley grinded onto his thick erection hungrily. She wanted to show him that she could handle him. Jamir put her other leg onto his shoulder and began pumping harder and faster into her. She took all his inches and moaned loudly.

"Mmm shit Jamir!"

"Yea. Ain't shit changed." Jamir said. He flipped Riley over and put her on top. She bounced on him until she began to squirt again.

"Damn girl, you like that dick, don't you?" he asked.

"Yes." Riley moaned.

Jamir grabbed a hold of her waist and took over. He pounded up into her ocean letting her juices rain down onto him. He didn't show her any mercy. He pulverized her until he busted a fat nut into the condom.

"Damn Jamir that dick is still good." she said as she climbed off him. Her box was throbbing from the beating Jamir gave it.

"That pussy is still good." he said. Riley giggled and laid next to him. They both passed out.

Chapter 5

Riley

Riley woke up the next morning to the sound of the birds chirping outside. She rolled over to put her arms around Jamir, but she felt nothing but sheets. Riley opened her eyes. Jamir was no longer in bed with her. She sat up straight in her bed and rubbed her eyes. She looked around her room. Jamir was nowhere in sight. Riley got out of bed, put on her robe, and walked to the living room. Candles were still lit. Food and wine was still on the table from the night before, but no Jamir. She looked towards the bathroom. Jamir wasn't in there either. Riley noticed that her front door was unlocked. Riley realized that Jamir left while she was sleeping. She felt a little irritation because

Jamir had left without telling her or saying goodbye. *What the hell.* she thought to herself. Riley began blowing out the candles that had burned until they were just liquid in the glass. She cleaned up the food that was left on the table. She poured the wine out of the wine glasses, rinsed them and put them in her dish washing machine. Riley rinsed the plates and silverware, and put them in dish washer machine also. She put the leftover lasagna in her refrigerator, and then she threw the leftover salad in the trash.

After Riley finished cleaning up, she went to her bathroom to run some bath water. She poured a little bubble bath liquid in the water. She went back to her bedroom and picked up her phone from the night stand to check her text messages. She hoped that there would be one from Jamir. A feeling of relief covered Riley when she saw that there was one text message notification. She hurriedly unlocked her phone and opened the message only to find that is was from her sister Raelyn. Riley read the text message from her sister, and then she dropped her phone onto her bed with an attitude. She didn't understand why Jamir would just leave. She felt that he could have at least woke her up to tell her that he had to go. Riley had never had a guy leave in the middle of the night. She thought about calling him to see why he left, but she chose to wait to see if he would call her.

Riley went back to her bathroom to turn off the bath water. She removed her robe and got in. The steamy hot water relaxed her as she rested her head on the wall behind her. Thoughts about how good sex with Jamir was the night before flooded her mind. The thoughts of him turned her on. She stepped out of the bathtub to grab her waterproof rabbit vibrator that Raelyn bought her out of her bathroom closet. She got back into the bathtub and closed her eyes. She put the buzzing, pink, toy on her clit. She leaned back and tried to get into the moment, but she couldn't focus. The vibrator felt good, but it wasn't giving her what she wanted, so she turned it off and set it on the side of tub. Riley decided to use her hand instead. She closed her eyes again and thought about Jamir as she began rubbing her fingers on her pearl. She rubbed her pearl in a circular motion and then she inserted two inside of her. She continued to think about Jamir and how he sucked on her peach the night before as she gave herself pleasure. Her orgasm came in no time. She let out a sigh of pleasure and bit her bottom lip when she reached her peak. Once the wonderful feeling of the orgasm subsided, she opened her eyes and sat up in the bathtub. Riley was pleased that she got hers, but it would have been better if Jamir was there to give her some morning time loving.

***

Later that day, Riley and Raelyn stopped by their parent's home for a visit. Raelyn pulled up right after Riley. Riley got out of her car and adjusted her jeans before walking over to hug her sister.

"It's kind of chilly today." Raelyn said when she hugged Riley.

"It's supposed to warm up later." Riley said as they walked up the sidewalk to their parent's home on the southside of Minneapolis.

"You know mom and dad are going to ask us about church." Riley said.

"I know. I don't want to hear it either." Raelyn said. They spent their whole lives in church, so when they got the chance to break away, the twins and their brother did so, quickly. They still go to church every now and then, but not as often as their parents would like them to.

"Hey!" Riley said when they walked in.

Their mom was in the kitchen cleaning and preparing food to cook for dinner. Their father came from the back room into the kitchen. He wrapped his arm around their mother's shoulders, kissed her on the cheek, and then he gave her a little pinch on the butt. Their mother shrieked and began laughing. Their father began laughing too. Their mother smacked their father on the shoulder and said, "You better stop that."

Their father said, "I can't help it. You're so beautiful baby."

Raelyn and Riley smiled at their parents. Riley loves how they still flirt with each other, even after twenty years of marriage. They always have love in their eyes when they looked at each other. Riley secretly wished that she had something like they had.

Their father smiled at their mother, then he walked over to the sisters and gave them warm hugs. He kissed both on their cheeks.

"You two look beautiful." he said.

"Thanks dad. You look nice." Riley said.

"Isn't your father fine?" Their mother asked playfully.

The sisters shook their heads and smiled.

"Oh, so y'all trying to say that I don't look good huh?" Their dad asked staring and smiling at Riley and her sister. He was standing with his arms open.

"Ok. Ok." He said while adjusting his suit jacket.

The sisters started laughing. "We didn't say that dad." Raelyn said.

Their parents are both almost fifty but can pass for thirty easy. Their mother had been mistaken as their sister many times. Their father works out and keeps his body very fit. His muscular arms are always visible through his shirts

"What brings you two by? Are both of you staying for dinner? Or do you have to work tonight?" Their mother asked.

"No, we are off tonight. We're staying for dinner." Raelyn replied as the twins sat down at the dining room table.

Their mom was standing in the kitchen still wearing her blazer and skirt suit she wore to work. She was wearing her house slippers. She hadn't even taken off her nylons yet. That was normal for their mom. She would get home get home from work and go straight to the kitchen to start preparing dinner. Their father still had on his suit and tie from work as well. He walked to the living room to turn on the television. Their father likes watching the news after work to catch up with current events. He removed his suit jacket, loosened his tie and sat down.

"What you two been up too?" he said loudly from the living room.

"Nothing." Riley said.

"Are you staying out of trouble?" he asked.

"Yes, we are." Riley responded.

"Where's your brother?" he asked.

"We don't know." Raelyn said.

"He hasn't been over here in while. When you talk to him, tell him to stop by and see his parents." he said.

"We will." Raelyn said.

"How's the job?" their mother asked.

"It's alright." Riley said.

"Just alright?" their mother asked.

"No, it's great." Riley said laughing. Raven started laughing with her. Their mother is always pressing her for more details. Riley had never been much of a talker. Even as a little girl, she was the quieter twin. Raelyn, on the other hand, couldn't keep her mouth closed. The only reason she wasn't talking so much at that moment was because she was preoccupied on her phone.

"When are you girls coming to church?" Their mom asked.

Raelyn looked over at Riley and pursed her lips.

"I don't know. Soon mom." Raelyn said and then she looked back down at her phone.

"What you been up to Raelyn?" Their mother asked. Riley nudged her shoulder to get her attention.

Raelyn looked up from her phone and said, "Stop." Raelyn pushed Riley back and then she said, "I've been working mom."

"Have you gotten back enrolled in school?"

"No not yet." Raelyn said.

"Don't waste too much time baby, you want to get in there, get that degree, and be done with it. Don't wait until you're in your forties. It's harder. Ask your dad."

"It is baby. Do it now. I had a hard time in school. I didn't realize that I had forgotten everything." he said.

"Riley, you're still in school, right?" he asked.

"Yes, I am." she said.

"Good. Don't quit. It will pay off. You can't be a bartender forever."

"I know." Riley said. Raelyn rolled her eyes up to the ceiling. She hated when their parents got on her about school.

"Stay focused." Their mother said to them while walking past. She lightly hit Raelyn with the dish towel she had in her hand. Their mom walked into the living room to hand their father a glass of water and a couple of pills, and then she turned and walked back towards the kitchen.

"Baby do you want sweet potatoes or mashed potatoes?" she called out to their father from the kitchen.

"Mashed potatoes." Their father called back. Their mom started washing and peeling some potatoes. Riley looked at her phone. No text message from Jamir. She rolled her eyes and set her phone down on the table.

"Mom would you like some help?" Riley asked. She knew that she needed to busy herself to take her mind off Jamir.

"Sure." her mom responded. Riley stood up from the table and walked into the kitchen. Raelyn went to go sit next to their father on the couch. Their mother handed Riley a potato and a peeler.

"How are things going?" she asked.

"They are alright."

"There you go with that word again."

Riley laughed. "Well what do you want me to say mom?"

"Nothing specific, just a little more than alright."

"Well, things are good. I have just been working."

"I am glad that you are still in school. I am not pressuring you, but I would like for that to be your focus so that you have something to fall back on."

"I know."

"Do you have a boyfriend yet?"

"No. Not yet."

"Are you a lesbian?"

Riley laughed and said, "No mom. I am not."

Her mom chuckled, "Well I have to ask."

"Mom when did you know daddy was the one?"

"Chile the day I met him. I just felt it. We were so young. Like you are now but we were in love. It wasn't easy. But we made it work. I knew that I could never be with another man."

Riley smiled at her mom. Seeing her parents made her yearn for the kind of love that they have. That everlasting love that is deep and withstanding. She wanted to walk down the aisle with the love of her life, have children, and live happily ever after one day. She wanted a man to look at her the way her father looks at her mother. Riley helped her mom peel the potatoes. Her mom put them in some water to begin boiling them. "Are you in the mood for my famous fried chicken?" her mother asked.

Riley said, "Yes."

She loves her mom's fried chicken, and was hoping that it will take her mind off Jamir. Riley was fighting the urge to text or call Jamir since he was the one who left and never said anything. She didn't understand why he hadn't called or text her yet either. It was late in the day and still nothing from him. After she finished helping her mom, she went into the living room and checked her phone. There was a text from Jamir.

I am sorry Riley. I had to get to work. I didn't wake you because you were sleeping so peacefully. I will call you later.

A smile spread across Riley's face. It was late in the evening, but she was happy to hear from him. She hurriedly sent a text message back to Jamir asking him if he could stop by later. When she got the text message back from him saying that he would be over, Riley went from being sad to happy immediately. She wasn't even interested in having dinner with the family anymore. Riley couldn't get it over fast enough, so she could get home to Jamir.

Her mom finished cooking the food in no time, but Riley felt like it took forever. She ate with the family and tried her best to keep her mind focused on the conversation, but her mind was already home figuring out what she was going to wear, and what needed to get straightened up around the house before Jamir got there. Once dinner was over, Riley didn't waste any time thanking her parents and telling them that she had to go. She hugged her parents and her sister and left out in a hurry.

Riley doesn't live far from her parents, so she made it home in ten minutes. She made a mad dash into the house after she parked her car. She made her bed, and remembered to hide her vibrator that she left beside the tub in the bathroom. She took a fast shower knowing that Jamir would be there any minute. Riley changed into a maxi dress without a bra or a pair of panties. The first thing on her agenda was to question why he hadn't called her. The second thing on her agenda was too get a repeat of that good good he gave her the night before. She had been thinking about having sex with him the whole ride home. Riley wanted a round two since he'd snuck out before giving her some that morning.

Riley rubbed shea butter on her body, and dabbed on a little vanilla scented oil. She sat on her bed and looked at the clock on her nightstand. It had been thirty minutes past the time Jamir said that he would be there, and he wasn't there yet. Riley walked out to her living room and sat down on her couch. She picked up her remote, turned on the television, and started watching Love and Hip-Hop Hollywood. She got half way into the program and realized Jamir still wasn't there. She picked up her phone, swiped the screen, and sent a text message.

Are you still coming?

She got a text back.

Be there in twenty minutes.

Thirty minutes past and still no Jamir. Riley checked her phone. No text message from Jamir either. By the time the one-hour program was going off, Riley was upset. Jamir still hadn't shown up.

"Uuuuugh." she thought.

Riley felt like she'd rushed home for nothing. She could have stopped over at Raelyn's place for a while. Riley stood up, crossed her arms in front of her, walked into her kitchen, and poured herself a glass of red wine. She sent Jamir another text message while walking back into the living room with her glass in hand.

I guess you are not coming.

Chapter 6

Riley

Riley woke up to the sound of her doorbell ringing. She looked around her apartment. All the lights were still on. She realized she had fallen asleep on the couch after she finished her glass of Merlot. She sat up and walked into her bathroom to gargled some mouth wash. After she spit it out, she wiped my mouth on a towel, and headed towards the door. She tip-toed down the stairs and looked out the curtain to see Jamir standing there. Riley rolled her eyes and unlocked the door.

"Hey baby." Jamir said when she opened the screen door.

"Nice of you to finally show up." Riley said and then she folded her arms over her chest.

"I got caught up baby I am sorry." he said.

"It's one o'clock in the morning Jamir." Riley said.

"Can I come in?" he asked.

Riley wanted to say no, but hell, he was looking sexy as hell to her with his baseball cap and bedroom eyes. She stepped back and let him in.

Once they were back upstairs in her apartment, Jamir said, "You mad? Com'ere." He grabbed her arm and pulled her to him.

"I mean, you leave out of here, I don't hear from you, then you come here at one o'clock in the morning, after telling me that you were going to be here in thirty minutes twice Jamir."

"I know. I got busy baby, but I was coming. You know I wasn't going to miss out on seeing your sexy ass." Jamir touched her face. When Riley felt his hand on her face, she felt weak and immediately softened up. Riley smiled and gazed into his eyes.

"Well you could have told me that you had to leave last night, and you could have told me that you were busy today." she whined.

"I know. I 'll do better baby ok?"

Riley replied, "Ok."

Jamir said, "You know I was thinking about you. I was thinking about getting some of that good you put on me last night."

Riley couldn't ignore how sexy and chocolate he was looking standing there in a camouflage wife beater, khaki shorts, and all white Adidas sneakers. Riley's eyes surveyed all his tattoos, and then she started kissing him and unbuttoning his pants.

"You want this D, don't you?" he asked.

"Um hum."

"Well get it then." he said.

Riley smiled and pulled his khaki shorts down over his butt a little just, so she could get to his long thickness. She bent down in front of him and looked directly at the smooth dark chocolate treat that she wanted to taste. It was already hard, so she didn't have to use her hands. She wrapped her soft lips around his thickness and began sucking it. She kept most of her focus on the head and only going a third of the way down on it.

"You can't fit all of it in there, can you?" he asked looking down at her and smiling.

Jamir pushed her head down on it as far as it could go. Riley began bobbing her head up and down on his thickness trying to swallow as much of it as she could. Jamir kept his hand on Riley's to push her towards his thrust into her mouth.

"There you go. Relax." he said as he grinded into her mouth. Once Riley was sucking him to his liking, he took his hand off her head and began rubbing himself as she sucked on him.

"You want me to taste that juice box again?" he asked while still stroking himself.

"Um hum." she hummed.

"Come on." he said.

Riley stopped, and Jamir helped her stand up. They walked over to her couch.

Jamir said, "Take that dress off."

Riley slid the dress down her body and let it drop to the floor. She watched him undress and then he lay on the couch on his back. Jamir told her to put it on his face. She climbed on top of him in a sixty-nine position. She took him into her mouth as he began licking on her peach. They went to work on each other kissing, slurping, licking, sucking, and pleasing each other. They stayed at it for a while and then Riley started losing control of her O. She could hear him losing control of his too and it turned her on even more. Riley moaned louder and then her orgasm hit her. Her body began shivering as she moaned his name and soaked his face with her juices. Jamir drank of her sweet nectar, and then he smacked her ass indicating that he wanted her to stand up.

Riley stood up and walked directly to her room. Jamir located his pants, pulled out a condom, met her in the bedroom, and flipped her over onto her stomach. Riley kept her upper body on the bed, but she placed her feet on the ground. She got up on her tip toes, so he could slide his long thickness into her from behind. Riley curved and arched her back for Jamir. He smacked Riley on her plump ass and proceeded to lay pipe to her. She bounced back a little until Jamir grabbed her hips and started pulling her to him. Riley stopped trying to give it back and started gripping her sheets. Jamir knew that he had her right where he wanted her. He was in control and she was on the brink of tapping out. Jamir kept her in that position until she screamed out that she couldn't take no more.

"Ahhh Jamir! I -Can't, I can-" Riley moaned breathlessly.

"Yes, you can." he responded while pounding into her. He pulled out, flipped her onto her back, and dove back into her like he was a professional diver. She winced and dug her nails into his back.

"Oh my-" she moaned out.

"Yea. Let that shit out."

"Ahhhh fuuuuck!" she groaned.

"Uh huh. You like that?" he asked staring into her eyes with his intense bedroom eyes. He pulled back and long thrusted her aggressively.

Riley squealed, "Yes!" She let go of his back and grabbed her sheets again. Riley started scooting backwards towards the headboard. It was a natural reaction to the pound game he was putting on her.

"Uh, uh. You tryna run again." Jamir said between pumps.

He put his hands under her ass and pulled her back to him. He closed her legs together and put her into a fetal position, and continued to lay pipe into her. He kept her in that position for a while and then he pushed both of her legs towards the headboard. Once he was done with that, he held both of her legs up by her ankles with one hand, and then he put her legs on his shoulders. He kept her legs on his shoulders while pounding his large tool into her until he busted.

"I'm about to bust baby." He groaned and then he busted into the condom. When it was all over, Riley was weak. She felt like she couldn't move. She could feel her kitty throbbing and her legs shaking. Jamir got up to flush the condom and wash up. He chuckled when he saw her still lying in the bed unable to move.

"Are you ok boo?" he asked. Jamir climbed back into her bed and pulled her into his arms.

"You know what you just did." she said.

Jamir chuckled, "You said you wanted it."

Riley giggled, "I see I need to careful what I ask for."

Jamir chuckled again and said, "That shit was good though."

"Yea. You put it down." she replied.

Jamir smiled. "Sexy ass was taking this dick."

"I almost tapped out." Riley said.

"I wasn't going to let you. You gonna learn how to handle this D. I am going to teach you." he said.

Riley laughed, nudged him, and then she asked, "Can you stay and not leave tonight?"

"Yes boo." Jamir said.

Riley cuddled into his arms. As she lay silently in Jamir's arms, she thought about how perfect the moment felt. Riley said a silent prayer that it would work out this time, and maybe they could get married like they should had before.

Chapter 7

Raelyn

"Come in!" I called out from my bedroom.

Riley opened the door and walked in. She closed the door behind her. I walked out of my bedroom.

"Hey sister!" I said and reached out to give Riley a hug.

We planned an old fashioned, all girls sleep over, at my apartment for our birthday. Everyone received an invitation and instructions in the mail. They were to wear pajamas and bring blankets and pillows. Riley had just come back. She had to go home and get changed. I told her to change at my place, but she had to be difficult. I was dressed in my one-piece Hello Kitty onesie. We decorated my apartment in colorful balloons, streamers, and confetti. We had party favors and snacks covering my coffee table, and there was lots of food in the kitchen on top of the stove and the counters. I had the latest hits playing from my mini speaker, and I was putting the finishing touches on everything when my sister made it back to my place.

Riley handed me a gift bag. "Happy birthday sister!"

"Thank You!" I exclaimed. I took the bag from her hand and I handed her a bag containing a present I had brought her.

"Thanks sis!" she said.

"Should we open them now or later?" I asked.

"Let's do it later." she said.

"Ok." We hugged and then walked to my bedroom to put the gift bags on my bed.

"I like your pajamas." I said.

She was dressed in a Sponge Bob two -piece pajama set. Riley sat down on the couch. I walked into the kitchen, opened the refrigerator, and pulled out the fruit punch bowl that we made earlier that day. We gutted a watermelon and then filled it with fruit and tons of liquor. The perfect antidote to get the ladies talking and telling all their secrets. I set the watermelon bowl on the card table I had set up in my living room.

"Do you think we made it too strong?" Riley asked as she walked over to the card table where I was standing.

"No." I said smiling.

"Look at that smile. You can't wait to get everybody drunk and telling their secrets, can you?" Riley asked laughing.

"You know it" I laughed with her. "I'm gonna get you telling your secrets right now." I said.

"Whatever." she said playfully.

"I'm serious. You gave him some, didn't you?" I asked.

"Huh? Who?" Riley asked smiling.

"Don't play me sister. You know who. Jamir that's who." I said.

Riley bit her lip and looked away.

"Oooo you let him get the cookie again Riley!" I said and then I smacked her on the ass.

"What?" Riley laughed.

"I knew you were going to do that." I said walking back into the kitchen.

"You know how I feel about him." Riley said.

"I know. How was it? Was it good?" I asked.

"Yes. Too good. It was amazing. You know he is very blessed in the lower region, and he gives good head." she said.

I said, "Oooo it's big? You never told me that."

"Yes, length and width."

"It's thick too?" I asked.

"Sis." She made a hand gesture to show his size.

"No."

"Um hum." She nodded her head.

"Wow. You never told me this before."

"I can't believe I didn't sis."

"You didn't. Oh well. I hope you used a condom." I said.

"I did."

"What about the wife?"

"He said that it was over and that he divorced her."

"Hmm. Ok." I said.

Riley said, "Now, it's your turn."

"For what?" I said.

"To tell your secrets."

"What secrets?"

"Laron. What's up with that?"

I paused and said, "Riley, he is wonderful."

"Oh yea?"

"Um hum."

"You're not just saying that because he ate the box on the first date, are you?"

"No. I like him, and we've been hanging out."

"Have *you* given him some yet?"

"Besides him tasting the cookie that night, no."

"Hasn't it been like two months? That is unusual for a man. He must be very patient."

"That's what I like about him. He isn't rushing."

"That's different."

"He is. He has come over a couple of times and cooked with me. The other day he helped me put together my new bookshelf. Tomorrow we are going out on a dinner date. I can't wait to see him again." I said. I was smiling the whole time and readjusting some of the decorations and party favors.

"Do you think that he might be the one?"

"I don't know yet, but part of me hopes that he is. I think I am ready to let him inside this flower bed."

"You're ready to let him dust the cob webs off that cookie after two years? He must be something." Riley said as she bit into a potato chip.

Someone knocked on my door. "Come in!" I yelled out. Our friends Taji and Cherry walked in.

"Hey twins! Happy birthday!" Taji said. Taji is tall, slim, and dark chocolate. Cherry is a little shorter than Taji and has more of a peanut butter complexion. She is heavier set than the rest of us and she wears it well. Cherry gave me and Riley a hug and handed me a gift bag.

"You guys didn't have to! Thank you!" I said. I took the gift bag from her hands.

"Make yourself comfortable, there is drink on the table and food in the kitchen."

"Heeey!" Cherry said as she headed towards the kitchen. Taji went straight to the table with the drink. Our cousins Michelle and Shanika arrived moments later. They were the last people that we were waiting for to get the party started. We filled up our plates with food, and everyone found somewhere to sit in the living room.

Once everyone was comfortable, I said, "Alright now that we are all here, let's get a game of 'I Never' started. Everybody fill your cups."

"What's that?" Taji asked.

"Well someone says that they never did something and if you did it, you have to take a drink." Cherry said.

"Ok. I'll go first." I said.

"I never had sex in a public place." I said. Everyone took a drink accept me.

"What? Sister!" I said to Riley and then I hit her in the arm.

"What?" she said while laughing.

"Ok. Y'all some freaks!" I said. Everyone started laughing.

"Who's going next?" I asked.

Taji said, "I will. Ok. I've never had a threesome." Cherry and Taji took a drink. Everyone started laughing.

"Oh, my God. Y'all had threesomes?" I asked.

"I did. With two guys. I liked it." Taji said.

"I did it once too. With another girl. It was the best sex I've ever had. You should try it once." Cherry said.

"I don't know about all that." I said.

"I'm not trying to share my D with nobody, and I don't need a chick to eat my cookie." Riley said.

"You don't know what you're missing." Cherry said.

"I think I agree with her another chick in the room is too much." Michelle said.

"What about two guys? Would you ever try that?" Taji asked.

"Now that's too many dicks in one room." I said. Everyone laughed out loud.

"Don't knock it until you try it." Taji said before we got back into playing the game and the rest of the night went per plan. Riley and I had the most fun we've ever had for our birthday. We usually go out to the club every year, but we wanted to do something different, and it turned out perfect. I got everybody to tell me their secrets, we ate good, we got extremely drunk, and then we all passed out everywhere in my apartment.

***

"How was your birthday party?" Laron asked me.

"It was fun."

"Yea? What did y'all do? Sit around and talk shit about men?"

"Something like that."

"Yea I know how you ladies get down when you get together." he said and then he smiled. I smiled back, picked up my fork, and took a bite of the tilapia on my plate. We were having dinner at a seafood restaurant Downtown Minneapolis. It was his birthday present to me along with some pretty earrings.

"I gotta fly out to Vegas in a few weeks. I was thinking about taking you with me. Do you think that you could come?

"Yes, I would love too."

We finished dinner and then we went to a hotel suite that he rented for my birthday. He assured me when he rented it that we didn't have to do anything there, but I had other things on my mind. I was ready to take our friendship to the next level. We'd been spending time with each other, but we hadn't done anything intimate since the first date. After I told him that I was celibate, he respected it and never made another sexual advance. He said that he was alright with building a friendship first before taking things to the next level. His patience made me want him more. I was ready to ditch my two-year sexual hiatus. He already showed me what his mouth could do. I was curious to see what that D could do too. Once we were in the room, he put a bottle of Cîroc on ice and made us both a drink. We both sat on the couch and talked for a while. When he made our second drink he sat down next to me and kissed me on the forehead.

"I hope that you are enjoying yourself." he said.

"I am. I love doing stuff like this. My job is so wild and busy at times that I've learned to cherish quiet and relaxed moments.

"I hear you. There is nothing wrong with kicking back. Everything doesn't have to be a party."

"Absolutely not." I said. We clinked glasses and took sips of our drinks.

"I like being around you. I like our vibe Raelyn." he said.

"I like you too." I said.

"Let's just chill tonight and do nothing. Is that cool?" he asked.

"Yes, that is cool." I said.

"Aight cool."

Chapter 8

Paris

"Spending the night out!? REALLY?" I said loudly. I was so angry with my husband for not coming home the night before. I didn't agree to that. That is not what I had in mind when I agreed to having a threesome with him.

"Stop tripping Paris. Nothing happened ok?" he said.

"So, you didn't have sex with her?" I asked him.

"No."

"Don't lie to me." I stood there with my arms folded across my chest. I was staring him directly in the eyes. He had been gone all night with Raelyn and I was livid. I knew that he was with her, but he didn't tell me that he was going to be with her all night. I'd called his phone multiple times throughout the night with no answer and no response.

"Baby nothing happened. Stop." He kissed me. I love my husband so much.

When I agreed to bringing another woman into our bed, I should have never told him he could pick the girl. We've been married for five years. He told me that he wanted to spice up our sex life and asked me if I was down. I had never been with a woman, but because I love him I agreed. It took me a while and a lot of his asking and convincing for me to agree to it. When I finally said that I would do it, he showed me a picture of her online. I thought she was pretty, so I let him pursue her. I even helped him pick out his outfit for the first date. I knew she would like him, my husband is fine as hell. He had my attention when I first met him, and I am picky. He got me with his light brown eyes. My husband's eyes are what most women like about him. He was always getting hit on by women and I was alright with it. My husband had never cheated on me, but every time he went out with her, I couldn't help but to wonder if he was pursuing her for our bed or just for him.

"Did you tell her about me yet?" I asked.

"No."

"Why Laron? Are you trying to have a girlfriend on the side?"

"No baby. I told you, I've been taking my time to get to know her first before I hit her with it."

"So, I am supposed to be a stupid bitch and wait while my husband has another relationship going on with another woman. That is not what I agreed to. You told me that you wanted to experience sex with two women and I was down with that, but you staying out all night is not ok."

"Baby I told you that I want it to be more than just sex. I want it to be an experience for all of us. I don't want to treat her like a piece of meat. If that was the case, we could have just gone out and picked up any chick from out of the club. I promise it will not happen again and I will tell her."

"You better, or I am going to tell her." I said while rolling my neck at the same time.

"Shut up." he said.

My husband was smiling at me. He grabbed one of my arms and pulled me to him. "Stop frowning and smile baby. I am not doing anything behind your back. I have told you everything that has happened thus far. It was her birthday, that is the only reason I stayed overnight. I was going to tell her last night, but I didn't want to kill the moment."

"Alright. Don't let it happen again Laron." I said.

He smacked my butt and then I turned and walked towards the kitchen to finish breakfast. My husband and I had a different kind of a relationship. He was like my best friend. We could talk about anything. The idea of doing something different sexually was his, but it isn't the first time we'd tried something different. We would attend these sex parties when we were first married. We never did anything at the parties, but we enjoyed watching others. We also recorded a lot of our sexual sessions when we got married. All of that was in the beginning. After a few years, our married life and sex life had gotten some what normal until he approached me about a threesome.

The first thing I said was, *"You're just trying to get permission to fuck another chick."*

He said, *"No I 'm trying to bring us a woman to have fun with."*

"Um hum whatever. I don't know."

"Well will you at least think about it for me baby?"

"Yea."

I thought about it for a while before he asked again. I pushed him off and he asked again. Finally, I told him yes, but he would have to choose the girl. I don't like girls, so I don't know what to look for. Seemed like he jumped on it quick because the next thing I knew, he was showing me a picture of Raelyn on social media. My first thought of her was that she was pretty. Looking through her pictures on social media, I noticed that she looked younger than us. Raelyn looked to be in her early twenties. She was brown skin with a nice body and a pretty smile. My husband and I were both thirty years old. I felt a little jealous.

"This is what he likes? So, I must be boring and old to him now." I said to myself.

I shook those thoughts from my head though. I'd never been insecure. I am a model, so beauty had never been my problem. I was not going to let some young chick come along and make me feel inferior. *My husband is mine and he is always going to be mine, no cute bitch is going to come in between that.* I thought to myself.

My husband sat down at the kitchen table while I finished cooking. I put a plate of food in front of him. I kissed him, and he smacked me on my ass again.

"I see you're in your workout clothes, are you getting ready for the runway show and photoshoot in Las Vegas?" he asked.

I replied, "Yes. I think this photoshoot and show is going to be awesome. I love this designer I am modeling for. His fashion is so amazing. I melt every time I put on one of his pieces."

"I know baby. Maybe he'll give you a piece to take with you like he did the last time." Laron said before taking a bite of his eggs.

"Hopefully, enjoy breakfast I am going to get dressed and meet up with Priscilla."

Priscilla is my best friend. We had been best friends for a few years. I hadn't told her about the arrangement that I made with my husband, but I wanted to talk to her about it to get some input. After I soaked in the bathtub, I put on a pair of jeans, a pretty blouse and some heels. I kissed my husband goodbye and left.

****

"You're married. Would you allow another woman into your bedroom?" I asked Priscilla

"I've had a threesome before I was married, and that was it. I don't like to share. Why are you asking me that anyway? Are you thinking about having a threesome with Laron?" she asked.

"Yes, I am, and I am not sure if I made the right decision."

"Well, I know how you two get down, but you got to be careful when you are bringing someone into your bedroom. My husband already knows it ain't happening with us. He better not even think, about asking me."

"I am open to experimenting with my husband because I love him, but girl he is pursuing this girl for the threesome, and he has been just doing too much."

"What? What do you mean pursuing?"

"I told him that he can find a girl and he did on social media. He's been kind of dating her, but she doesn't know about me yet."

"Whoa Paris. You are letting you husband date another woman? You are crazy."

"I am with a man who is good looking and has a job that requires him to be around beautiful women all the time. I guess I am just used to him being around women."

"Yes, but being around women for work and actually dating a woman are two different things. Damn girl you will practically do anything for that man."

"Not anything."

"Yes, girl anything. Maybe you don't see it."

"I guess."

"Well, good luck with that girl, but be careful. Love triangles can get complicated.

Chapter 9

Raelyn

I parked my car behind the club and hopped out rocking form fitted, V-neck, Purple Rain t-shirt with a pair of black jeggings, and a pair of black Chuck Taylor's. My hair was pulled back into a ponytail. I walked through the backdoor of the club and waved hello to the owner as I walked past his office and then I walked to the backroom where all the staff hung out before club opening.

I said "Yo!" when I walked in the door. A few of the Bouncers were there and a couple of the other bartenders were sitting around.

One of the bouncers said, "What up Raelyn."

He was the one that has had a crush on me for a while. Shawn was cute, but he wasn't really my type. He didn't have that athletic build that I like. Very surface of me, but true. It's hard to be into someone when the physical attraction isn't there. Shawn seemed to have a good head on his shoulders based on few short conversations that I had with him.

I spoke to him and sat down in one of the metal fold out chairs. I pulled out a small mirror to check my make-up. I had my purple glitter shadow popping to match my t-shirt and nude colored lipstick. The club owner prefers that all the staff wear black, but he allows the ladies to add a pop of color which I do quite frequently. Riley walked in moments later smiling. She was rocking all black with hot pink lipstick on her lips.

"Yo!" she said. Everyone said hi as she walked over to kiss me on the cheek.

It was Thirsty Thursdays which meant drinks were two dollars until eleven o clock. It was going to be complete chaos for the first 2 hours and then straight madness afterwards because everyone would be stupid drunk. Especially if they come to my bar because I know how to make the drinks right. I don't use the bottles that have water in them like the club owner wants us to use. I make real drinks and that is why my tips stay fat.

"What's up sister? Are you ready for this craziness tonight?" I said to Riley.

"As ready as I'll ever be." she said.

Both of us locked our purses up in lockers. We walked to the bar to make sure everything was set up at the one we were working at. We wanted to make sure that the glasses were clean, and that we had enough to get us through the rush. I know the bar-back will keep us stocked but sometimes they get behind depending on who it is for the night. We checked to make sure our bottles were full or close to it, and that we had towels around for occasional spills. Everything looked good and it was time for the club to open.

Only a few people trickled in at club opening. My first order was for a few lemon-drop martinis. Early arrivers always seem to be the most laid back. I nodded my head to the music the DJ had going and kicked back waiting for the rush. An hour later more people were coming in. I poured a few glasses of wine and then it was on. A ton of appletini's, a bunch of Hennessey shots, several long island ice teas, Heinekens, Coronas, Fire ball shots, Patron shots, Cîroc shots, Cherry bomb shots, and a bunch of other drinks later. My night was over, and I had three hundred dollars in my pocket. Riley had about the same amount. As the bouncers ushered the crowd out of the club, Riley and I cleaned the bar. We joked and laughed about some of the people that got put out of the club because they couldn't handle their liquor.

"Did you see the dude in the white shirt?" Riley asked.

"Yea he was sliding all on the ground. I guess he thought he was dancing." I said while laughing. I looked up to see Laron standing by the bar waiting to get my attention.

"Hey." I smiled at him and he smiled back. He was looking good, but he had his grill in. I planned to tell him that I hated that thing one day.

"I'll meet you by your car ok?" he said.

"I said ok."

He turned and walked back out of the club. "Girl he is too fine, but what is he doing here?" Riley asked.

I said, "I don't know. I guess to surprise me. He didn't tell me that he was coming."

Riley smiled and put away the last glass.

"You give him some yet?" she asked.

"No."

"What are you waiting on?"

"I thought about it, but we both agreed that we wanted to take our time."

Riley nodded her head that she understood as we walked to the backroom to get our things. We talked about Jamir a little bit on our way back there. She said that everything was going fine between them, and that they'd been spending a lot of time together, but there were still some days when he didn't call her. I told her that I felt something wasn't right about that, but she was so gone over him, and she refused to listen to me. I let her explain to me the reasons why his disappearing was alright. It all sounded like excuses to me, but she's grown, so I didn't fight with her about it.

"He is perfect for me Rae." she said.

"Why do you think that?"

"Because it's just the way I feel." Riley said as we were walking out of the club.

"Ok." I said as I hugged her goodbye. She walked to her car and I walked over to Laron who was standing by my car. He spoke to Riley and hugged me.

"How was work?" he asked.

"It was a good night, but what are you doing here?"

"I just wanted to see you, so I stopped by."

"Aw you missed me already?" I asked flirtatiously.

"I really did." he said.

I asked, "You want to come by my place for a little while?"

He said, "Yea. I'll follow you in my car."

Laron opened my car door for me, so I could get in. Once I was in and had my car started, he got into his and followed me home. I was excited to see him and get a chance to spend some time with him. Since that night at the hotel, he'd gotten busy with work and hadn't been able to hang out as much. He had to take a couple of trips out of town. I knew that he had just gotten back into town earlier in the day, but I wasn't expecting to see him. I figured that he would be trying to rest up.

We made it to my house in no time. I pulled into the parking garage connected to my apartment building as Laron found parking on the street. I met him at the front door to let him into the building. I took my shoes off at the door after entering my apartment and put them on the mat next to the door. Laron did the same and followed me into the living room. He sat down on the couch and I walked towards the kitchen.

"Would you like something to drink? I have water and juice."

"Water is fine." Laron said.

I walked from the kitchen to the living room with a bottle of water in my hand. I handed him the bottle of water and told him that I would be right back. I headed to my bathroom to take a shower. I can't stand to feel sweaty after running back and forth behind the bar all night. Laron was respectful enough to stay and chill in the living room while I got cleaned up. He has done it many times before.

I stepped into the steamy hot shower. The hot water felt like a million warm rain droplets falling on to my skin. I could have stayed in the shower for an hour, but I didn't want to be rude to my company. After I finished cleaning my body with my favorite aroma therapy soap, I stepped out of the shower and dried off. I wrapped a towel around me and walked out of the bathroom into my bedroom. I sat on the bed and started applying lotion to my feet and legs. Laron knocked on the door. He had to know that I was wrapped in a towel. He probably wanted to catch me that way. Secretly, I wanted him to see me in my towel because I felt like I was looking sexy in a towel after my shower.

I looked up and said, "Yes?"

Laron peeked his head through a crack in the door. I smiled as I looked him over. He was dressed casually in a black t-shirt and a pair of black jogging pants. He had his dreads pulled back into a ponytail. Honestly, if he wanted me right then, he could have had me.

"Want me to put some lotion on your back?"

"Sure." I responded. I walked out of the bathroom and sat on the edge of my bed.

He sat down next to me. I moved the towel down enough for him to rub some lotion on the top half of my back without me exposing my whole naked body. He kissed my shoulder a couple of times as he began gently massaging them. I immediately reposed under the gentle squeezes to my shoulders.

"How does that feel?" he asked.

"Good." I said with my eyes closed and head slumped forward. I felt his hands work their way up the back of my neck.

Laron said, "You deserve this after a long night at work."

"Thank you." I said. I felt another kiss on my shoulder. The kiss sent shivers through my body that mixed with the relaxing sensation of his shoulder massage. I felt like I was in a trance. He had me right where he wanted me.

"Let me taste you again." Laron whispered into my ear.

"Huh?" I asked him. I heard him. I just didn't know what else to say.

"Lay back." I instantly started to feel self-conscious. I'd never done anything with a man with all the lights on. I'd never had a man looking directly at my peach unless in the dark and most of the time under the covers. Even in the parking garage that night of our first date it was dark, and I was wearing a dress. Plus, I was drunk, so I was feeling a little bodacious. I laid back onto my bed still holding my towel closed. He bent down in front of me, opened the bottom half of my towel, and kissed my inner thigh. He looked up at me. *Damn he fine.* I thought to myself. But I couldn't help the shy feeling

"Relax, let me see you," he said. I slowly let go of the towel. He lifted one of my legs and slowly kissed my inner thigh down to my peach. He lightly blew on it before kissing my lower lips. As soon as I felt his tongue on my pearl, I was in heaven. Laron knows what he is doing when it comes to pleasing a woman. As I moaned and grabbed my sheets, he gave me the best thirty minutes of oral pleasure I've had since the night in his truck. I almost told him that I loved him when I had my orgasm. Although I was ready to feel him inside me, he didn't try to have sex with me. He went into my bathroom to clean himself up, and then he laid next to me and cuddled with me in my bed.

***

Later that night, we lay in my bed cuddling, talking, and getting to know each other a little more. So far, since we've met, he had told me that he was born and raised in Minneapolis, Minnesota on the northside. One of the most popular black communities in the state, but known for being crime ridden in some parts. He was raised by a single hard-working mom. He is the oldest, but is now the only child because his younger brother was shot and killed. His love for photography started while he was in high school. He was always the designated photographer at family events when they needed someone to take a group picture. That is when he realized that he loved to take pictures, so he would take pictures of everything with his mother's camera until she bought him one of his own. He began telling me about more of his photography experiences while we laid in my bed chilling.

"I remember this one model I did a shoot for; her breath was too foul, and she was fine too. The whole time I was shooting her pictures I kept thinking how are you a top model with stinking ass breath." I laughed at what he said.

"I've been in this business a long time and I've seen a lot."

"Is your job the reason why you are single?" Up until then I hadn't really asked about his dating life. Not since our first date which was months prior. That was when he told me that it was complicated. I took that answer not sure of what was to come, but I probably should have probed more.

"What do you mean?" Laron asked me.

"Being around women all the time, does that make you not want to be in a relationship?" He smiled and looked at me with those light brown eyes.

"Well, Raelyn. I've been wanting to talk to you about that."

"About what?"

I figured maybe he wanted to know where this thing was going with us since it had been a few months that we had been dating. I just knew that he was probably going to explain that he likes to chill, but wasn't looking for anything serious. I braced myself for the blow. I was feeling him, so I knew I would have to get my feelings in check right away.

"Well, um, I've been trying to figure out the right time to talk to you. I just haven't wanted to kill the vibe because I really like you. It has been hard for me to find the right way to say this."

"Say what?"

"That, I am married." he paused and then I paused.

Did he just say what I think he said? No, he didn't say the M word, did he? I questioned myself. My face frowned and I snapped.

"Married!?" I sat straight up and looked at him like he had shit on his face.

"Raelyn wait, don't get upset." he said.

"Don't get upset!? Explain this to me! Your married like how?! Married like common law marriage? Married like separated and getting a divorce!? What kind of married?" I stared at him; waiting for an answer.

"Married like happily married, but my wife is ok with this."

"What the fuck!?" I yelled. "What wife is going to be ok with her husband dating another woman!? I can't believe that I've been dating a married man!" I scooted away from him and got out of my bed on the other side.

"Raelyn, I promise you it's not what you think. Give me a chance to explain before you blow up."

"No! I don't fuck with married men! Get out!" I pointed towards the door.

I was so upset that my chest felt tight. Laron didn't try to explain anymore. He got out of my bed and walked towards the front door. He put on his shoes and left. As soon as he left, I found my cell phone and called Riley. I needed to talk to my best friend.

Chapter 10

Riley

Riley heard her phone ringing, but she was in the middle of getting some thug loving from Jamir. Riley's legs were above her head and Jamir was beating it up for real. She was screeching in high octaves and digging her nails into his back when her phone started ringing. Jamir pulled out and then gave her an aggressive thrust. She yelped "Oh my God!"

"Yea you like that don't you?" he said while still thrusting in and out of her at a fast pace.

"Yes!" she moaned.

"Yes what?"

"Yes Jamir!"

"Say my name again."

"Jamir!" she moaned loudly. He was staring down at her with his sexy, slanted, deep brown bedroom eyes.

She loved seeing his brown skin was glistening with sweat. Riley's brown skin was glistening with sweat too. He pulled out again and flipped her over onto her stomach. Jamir pulled her hips up. She adjusted onto her knees and arched her back for him. He entered her from behind and smacked her ass hard.

"Whose is this?" he asked.

"Yours!" she said loudly.

"That's right!" Jamir growled and then he smacked her ass again.

The sound echoed through her bedroom. Riley hoped that her downstairs neighbors couldn't hear her. She grabbed the closest pillow and buried her face in it. Jamir grabbed Riley's hair pulled her head back towards him.

"Uh-uh. Let that shit out." he growled while pumping aggressively into her. Riley shrieked. Jamir had got on some Trey Songz stuff and wanted the neighbors to know his name. He was deep in her ocean and she was close to her O. When Jamir heard her scream, he began pumping harder and faster.

"Shit!" she squealed.

The sound of him smacking her backside again echoed through her room. Riley's headboard was knocking against the wall with every single one of his thrusts. Jamir was not letting up and Riley was loving every moment of it. She bit into another pillow, shrieked, and froze as her orgasm took over. They heard a few thuds on her floor. Riley's neighbors were banging something on their ceiling.

"Shit they can hear us. Stop Jamir." she whispered to him.

"Uh-uh." he said. Jamir kept pounding into Riley and her headboard kept knocking on the wall.

"Stop." she whispered to him again.

"Let them mutha fucka's call the cops." he said as he plunged deep again.

"Shit!" Riley whispered loudly. Jamir kept pounding until he exploded.

"Uh! This pussy good!" he said loudly. He held onto her hips until he released all his seeds into the condom, and then he pulled out and laid next to her. Riley's body felt limp as she flipped over onto her back. She was lying next to him trying to catch her breath. Jamir got up and went into the bathroom. Riley heard the sink water running and the toilet flush, and then she heard her bathroom closet open and close. Jamir stepped out of the bathroom a few minutes later zipping up his jeans.

"I got to go." he said.

Riley's face screwed, "Why?" she asked. Riley

looked at the clock. It was only a little after ten o'clock at night.

"I got some stuff to take care of. Don't look at me like that. I'll call you later." he said.

He pulled his Nike t-shirt over his head. Riley slid out of bed with her bed sheet wrapped around her naked body and walked Jamir to the door. He turned and kissed Riley on the cheek and then he left. Riley was pissed. That was the second time that he had left right after sex. He knew that she didn't like when he did that. Jamir knew that Riley wanted him to spend the night, but he always seemed to have something to do.

It had been several months, and Jamir hadn't so much as told Riley he was at least thinking about being in a committed relationship with her. Riley wasn't trying to rush, but she wanted to know if there was going to be something more in the future, or if sex was all that it was going to be. Riley had already told him how she felt about him. She told him that she was looking for more, and that she could see a future with him, but he never responded the way she wanted him to. Every time they had sex, she felt more addicted to him. Riley felt like she was becoming obsessed with making him commit to her. In her mind, they would have made the perfect couple, but he kept holding back. He would always shy away from the conversation, or tell her to chill out.

"I am feeling you alright? You ain't got to get so deep all the time. Just chill boo. Let everything be what it is and happen naturally" is what he told Riley the last time she started asking him about the status of their relationship.

Riley walked with her bed sheet still tied around her from the door to the kitchen. She poured a shot of patron over a cup of ice and took a sip. Riley remembered that Raelyn had called her. She knew that Raelyn was going to know that she was having sex because Riley never misses her calls. Riley walked into her room, set her glass down on the night stand, picked up her cell phone, and sat on the edge of the bed. She tapped the screen to dial Raelyn's number.

"Yo chick, you must have been getting some D, weren't you?" Raelyn said when she answered the phone. Riley sucked her teeth.

Raelyn laughed and said, "Don't lie."

"I was." Riley said.

"Ewww you nasty. Is he still there?"

"No."

"What? Where is he?"

"He had something to do, so he had to leave."

"Oh. It must have been pretty important."

"I guess it was." Riley took a sip of my Patron shot, and then she asked, "What's up with you girl?"

"I am so pissed right now. I am not talking to Laron ever again!" Raelyn said angrily.

"What happened? I thought that you were feeling him?"

"I was girl until he told me that he was married!"

"What!? No!"

"Yes!"

"When?!"

"Tonight, after he finished making me scream his name from his tongue!".

"He is married and eating your cookie?"

"Yes!"

"You mean like married and separated, right?"

"No like married and still together!"

"Get the fuck out of here!"

"Sister!"

"So, what did you do?"

"I told him to get out!"

"Oh my God. That's that bullshit right there."

"I know. I am so mad and embarrassed right now. You know I don't mess with married men."

"I know. Me either. Now, what are you going to do?"

"I am never talking to him again. I already blocked his number. Forget that."

Chapter 11

Raelyn

I adjusted my off the shoulder sweater as I walked with Riley out the back door of the club. It was a busy night at the club. Everyone who was anyone came out to our brother's "End of The Summer" party. Riley and I made cake; meaning lots of money. Summer was over, and fall was beginning. Kids and college students were going back to school. The smell of dying leaves and fire places filled the air as the weather started to cool down heading into winter. Riley and I were both rocking knee-high boots with no heels. I had on a pair of leggings with my off the shoulder sweater. Riley was rocking a sweater dress.

We exited the club into the alley/parking lot behind the club. We stopped short when we saw a fight getting ready to happen in the middle of the street. It was three o'clock in the morning and two guys were arguing back and forth outside of the club. It's ridiculous how people get after a few too many drinks. We stopped to watch with the other onlookers to see what was going to happen, but a few cops showed up on horses to clear the crowd.

Riley and I turned around and headed towards our cars. That's when we saw Laron standing by my car. Riley raised her eyebrows and looked at me. "How are you doing, Riley?" Laron said to her and gave her a short wave.

"Hey Laron, I'm good." she said. She turned to give me a hug. As I hugged her, she whispered to me, "Are you ok sis? Do you need me to stick around?"

"No. I am ok."

"Are you sure?"

"Yes."

"Alright love you." she said.

"I love you too." I said. We released one another from our hug. She walked to her car and I walked over to mine. I gave him eye contact and then I rolled my eyes. He was standing at the back of my car. I walked past him to the driver side door.

"So, you're not going to speak to me?" he asked.

He was looking so good. His salmon colored lips

looked softer than before. He had his sandy brown dreads hanging lose around his shoulders underneath a fitted baseball cap, and he was wearing a pair of clear Ralph Lauren frames on his eyes. He had on a letterman's jacket over a tight fitted t-shirt that showed off his muscular frame. *Calm down.* I thought. I was speaking to my throbbing pearl. I wanted him instantly, but I refused to show it. He was married which meant I was going home to my beloved vibrator.

"What are you doing here?" I asked without giving eye contact. I proceeded to open my car door to get in.

"I miss you and I feel like we should talk Raelyn. You don't fully understand, and I want to explain." he said walking towards the driver's side of the car.

"Explain what? There is nothing left to explain. You are married, and I am done." I got into my car. He adjusted his jeans and letterman's coat and kneeled next to me in the open car door.

"Raelyn you're over reacting. It's not what you think. Can you at least allow me to take you to breakfast, so we can talk?"

I put the key into the ignition and started the car. I looked at him. His tan skin was glowing underneath the moon and the street lamps. *Uuugh why does he have to be so fine? Why couldn't be an ugly dude so I can pull off on his ass without a care.* I thought. Instead of closing the door and pulling off, I turned to him and paused.

"Please?" he begged. He was giving me puppy dog eyes.

I gave in and said, "Alright, breakfast, that's it."

Laron smiled and clapped his hands together. "Cool follow me to the breakfast spot on Hennepin Avenue in Uptown."

Laron stood up and I watched him walk to his car. I loved how smooth and confident his walk was. When he pulled out of the parking space, I pulled out and followed him out of the alley/parking lot towards the street.

We arrived at the twenty-four-hour restaurant a few minutes later. We walked in the greasy spoon and found a seat. The place was packed with a bunch of drunken club goers trying to sober up before driving home. Laron and I grabbed a booth by the window. After we ordered drinks, we ordered food. I ordered an omelet and hash browns; he ordered steak and eggs. While we sipped on orange juice, he started the conversation.

"Let me start with saying this. It was never my intention to lie to you."

"But you did."

"I kept out some details."

"Omitting is a form of lying."

"I know I should have told you sooner, but I didn't want to run the risk of you running away."

"Marriage is need to know information."

He slightly chuckled and said, "Raelyn, yes I am married-"

"Ok. So why are we here?" I asked.

"Because I am interested in you. My wife knows that I am interested in you and she is ok with that."

"You're gonna keep lying to me?"

"I can call her right now and she will tell you. She knows that I am here."

"Basically, you guys are some swingers."

"No." Laron laughed.

"So, what is it then?"

"I have never wife swapped with another man and I never will. My wife and I are very open with each other, and I expressed to her that I was interested in having another lover, and she said that she was ok with it and then I saw you on social media."

"You stalked me?!" I leaned back into the leather booth cushions behind me and crossed my arms.

"No Raelyn. I was going to send you a message on

social media to ask you on date. It was a coincidence that we ended up at the same party and had similar acquaintances. I recognized your face when Jamir introduced us. I was like this is the girl I've been wanting to meet."

"Did your wife know about you meeting me there."

"No. She was actually supposed to be with me, but she changed her mind at the last minute."

"This is crazy." I said and took a sip of my orange juice. He took a sip of his as well and then our waitress arrived with our food.

"I know this sounds crazy, but it's real. No drama, no lies, no games, no one else. I'm telling you that I have feelings for you and I really want to be with you."

"You have a wife."

"Don't worry about her. She's with it."

"I asked you this before. What woman is ok with her man dealing with another woman?"

"Mine."

"I can't."

"Look, don't run away from it because it's different. Open your mind to something new. You will never know if you like it if you don't try it. Just try it.

"How many women have you two done this with?"

"None. Just you. I want you. Nobody else. I'm telling you. It's the perfect situation. You will not be disappointed. Just give it a chance and if you don't like it you can walk away."

I put my fork down. "I can't Laron." I whispered."

After we took a few bites of our food Laron asked, "Why?"

"I don't like women. I have never been with a woman."

"You're feeling me, right?"

"Yes. I was."

"Stop it," he smiled. "You still are."

"Whatever."

"Babe you don't have to touch her, and there is no rush." he said while staring into my eyes. I took a deep breath and exhaled. I took another bite of my food.

"I promise that you will like it babe." Laron reached out and touched my hand. I looked up from my plate and into his green eyes. I was at a loss for words.

I took a deep breath and then I said, "I don't know Laron. I don't believe that is something that I can do."

"Will you at least meet her? See how you feel

then?" he asked.

"I don't know."

"Think about it."

Chapter 12

Raelyn

I laid in my bed later that morning, trying to pleasure myself, but I couldn't seem to keep myself in the mood. My mind was on Laron and what he told me. I had never been approached about something like that before. He was right. Maybe I do need to open my mind and try something new. I mean hell, I am young, and I will only live once. I had already spent two years being a prude. *What could it hurt? If I don't like it, I can always walk away. They are the ones who are stuck with each other. Plus, he said I didn't have to touch her, and if I do it, I'm not going to.* I thought.

How could I tell Riley that I was contemplating dating a married man and his wife? I could hear her freaking out about the whole thing. I needed someone to talk to, so I put my vibrator away and called up my girl Taji. I asked her to come to the salon with me, I'll run it past her and see what she thinks about it before I talk to Riley.

***

I made it to the salon later that afternoon. I go to a salon called Sasha's. Sasha, the salon owner, is known in the city for slaying and laying hair. Some of the best stylists in the city work in her salon. Since I got my hair done at Sasha's, I have never gone to another place. I made an appointment weeks ago to get my hair weaved. My appointment was set to see Tamika. Sasha was already booked months' out.

I was already in Tamika's chair when Taji made it. Tamika told Taji that she could sit in the empty station that separated her station from Sasha's. The stylist that used that station was off for the day.

"Sorry I am late." Taji said when she sat down in the swivel stylist chair.

"It's ok."

"Hey Sash!" Taji said to Sasha

"Hey Taji!" she said as she was putting spiral curls in her client's hair.

Anthony also known as Anya said, "Heeey!" as he turned his client towards him to cut their bangs. Anthony is just like one of the girls.

"Hey Anya!' Sup with you?" Taji asked.

"Girl you know, I'm living. How you been Taji? Sitting over there looking like a tall glass of chocolate milk." Anya said. Everyone in the salon laughed.

Taji is tall, slim, with a dark chocolate complexion, and slanted deep brown eyes. She usually wears a long jet-black weave combed straight back, and hanging long to her butt. She never wears bangs, or her hair around her face. If it isn't hanging loose, then it is in a ponytail. She has flawless skin and wears minimal make-up.

Taji said. "You so crazy! I have been good."

Tamika flicked the client cape she had in her hand in the air. The cape made a whoosh sound as it went up in the air. She wrapped the cape around my shoulders and tied it in the back of my neck. I adjusted the cape over my arms and legs. Tamika took the rubber band that was holding my hair into a ponytail out. My hair released into a curly afro. She rubbed her hands through my hair and scalp then she said, "Come on."

I followed her to the shampoo bowls. I sat down in the black leather chair and put my head back into the shampoo bowl. I made myself comfortable as Tamika adjusted the water for my shampoo. Once Tamika had the water to a nice temperature, she sprayed a little in my hair to test the water on my scalp.

Tamika asked, "How does that feel?" She had the temperature just the way I like it.

I said, "Great."

I closed my eyes and got lost in the feeling of Tamika shampooing my hair. She scrubbed my scalp with her fingers, then she massaged my scalp. I was in heaven. I felt my head relax and then my body. Just when I felt like I was going to fall asleep, Tamika turned the sink off and started pat drying my hair with a towel. I opened my eyes. The three minutes of pure bliss was over too quickly.

"Tamika girl the way you shampoo is amazing." I said.

Tamika laughed and said, "Thanks."

She walked me over to the dryers and asked me to sit down. She set the timer and pulled the hood of the dryer over my head. Tamika walked away and left me under the dryer, so my hair could get deep conditioned. While I was sitting under the hooded dryer, I took my phone out of my sweater pocket and logged into my social media app. As I scrolled through my timeline, a text message came through from Laron.

Hey Beautiful. Can I see you later?

I felt butterflies in my stomach when I saw the text. I started thinking about what we talked about that morning. I just couldn't get over the fact that he had a wife, and that she was alright with him dating me, and then to also want to be involved with the both them as well. What kind of craziness is that? I started to wonder what she looked like. Was she tall, short, fat, or skinny? Was she African American? Was she pretty or ugly? She might be ugly and that is the reason why she allows her husband to do what he wants. I text messaged Laron back and told him that he could see me. It was my night off.

Tamika came back to get me from the dryer after about fifteen minutes. I followed Tamika back to her chair. After she blow dried my hair out she began putting corn rolls in it to set the foundation for my weave to be sewn in. As she was corn rolling my hair, she engaged in some light conversation with me and everyone who was in the salon.

"Oh Sash, I meant to tell you. Do you remember that girl that used to come in here with the twins a long time ago?"

"Yes Briana, she was engaged to Bryan." Sasha said.

"I remember her." Anya said.

"Briana Taylor?" I asked.

"Yep that's her." Tamika said.

"I went to high school with her. I haven't seen her in a long time."

"What happened?" Sasha asked.

"I saw on the news today that there was a shooting outside of a nightclub, involving Bryan, Briana, and her new husband." Tamika said.

"You're lying." Sasha said as she turned her client towards her. She stopped moving and looked at Tamika.

"No, I'm not. They didn't have any details this morning, but I hope that she is ok."

"Oh my God." Sasha said.

"I hope she was the one shooting him because I heard that he used to be putting his hands on her and shit, and you know I don't play that." Anya said. "Excuse my language," he said to his client.

"Uh- Uh" I said.

"I heard the same thing too Anya, and I often wonder if that was the reason she stopped coming here. I knew something was wrong." Sasha said.

"They seemed so happy." I said.

"Everything isn't always what it seems." Sasha said.

"Didn't you say the last time she was in here she asked to use the phone and then left?" Anya asked.

"Yup, she looked mad when she left too. That's such sad news Tamika, I hope that she is ok." Sasha said while looking in the mirror at her client. She was putting the finishing touches on the hairstyle she had just finished.

"I do too. I said."

After about an hour and half, all the other clients had left. Only me, Taji, and the stylists were left in there. It was almost time for closing and Tamika was a little over hallway done with sewing the eighteen-inch Brazilian wavy tresses into my hair. Sasha was sitting in her chair cleaning her tools. Anya was in his chair looking down at his phone; probably checking one of his social media pages.

I said, "Since we are all in here alone, I have a question for y'all."

"Sup?" Tamika asked.

"Have you ever had a threesome?" I asked.

Anya looked up from his phone. "I can't believe little miss prissy Raelyn is asking something like that. What the hell?"

I laughed and blushed. "I am just asking. Have you?"

"Uh-uh" Tamika said.

"What kind? Another girl or two guys?" Sasha asked.

"I've done two guys before. I mean y'all know that I'm a freak." Anya said. I giggled.

"I haven't, but my ex-husband wanted me to with another girl. I just couldn't pull myself to do it. Something about it made me feel like he just wanted permission to cheat on me." Sasha said.

"You know that I have." Taji said.

"Girl or guy?" Tamika asked

"Both." Taji said.

"Oh, my God Taj! You didn't say that at my party" I said and chuckled.

"I know, but I didn't want to tell all my business." she laughed and blushed.

"I never knew you were like that!" I laughed.

"Whaaaaat." she sang. "I like to try things."

"That's ok Taji boo. You a freak like me." Anya said.

"Why though Raelyn? Are you thinking about having a threesome?" Taji asked.

"Maybe." I said.

"Wooow!" Sasha said.

"You're just coming all out of your shell these days Ms. Prissy huh?" Anya said.

"What made you want to do that?" Tamika asked.

"Someone that I am currently dating asked me." I said.

"That someone wouldn't be the dude we met at Eazy's party, would it?" Taji asked.

"Maybe." I said.

"Well he was fine, and we are grown so Yolo." Taji said.

"What does yolo mean?" Sasha asked.

"It means You Only Live Once. Why not have fun and experience things? We are young. We are supposed to be free. As long as you protect yourself. I would do it." Taji said.

I twiddled my thumbs, "Hmmmm. I don't know. I might."

Chapter 13

Paris

I was kind of relived when Laron told me that he and Raelyn weren't talking, but he had the nerve to be frustrated. I didn't like that. I mean he was acting like that chick was all that. It was supposed to be fun, but I wasn't feeling him liking someone else on that level. I told him that I was good on the whole thing, but he went right back to chasing her down. I was so irritated that I had to take a shot of Vodka just to calm down.

As I took a few deep breaths, I sat down on our red couch and tried calling Laron again. No answer. I put my phone on the glass coffee table. I crossed one leg over the other and started bouncing it up and down, then, I crossed my arms over my chest. I couldn't stop bouncing my leg, so I stood up and paced back and forth, and then I went over to the window and looked out of it. Laron really had me fucked up with the stunts that he kept pulling.

"I should have never told him yes. Now, he thinks he can do whatever he wants." I said out loud to myself. I walked from the living room back to the kitchen. I poured another shot of Vodka. I opened the cabinet that I had my cigarettes hidden in. I grabbed the pack, a lighter, and the ashtray that I had washed out and hidden away. I usually smoke outside, but my nerves were so bad I decided to smoke in the house. I walked back to the couch, sat down, took my shot, and lit my cigarette.

A feeling of relief rushed over me as I blew the smoke out. I was supposed to be quitting, but the way my husband had me feeling made me flush my three weeks without cigarettes down the drain. I am not a heavy drinker, but I love my cigarettes. Laron had me doing two things that I wasn't trying to do at all. I leaned back onto the couch with my legs and arms crossed enjoying the tingly sensation that the nicotine was giving me. When I finished that cigarette, I tried to call Laron again. When he didn't answer, I sent him an angry text message.

WHERE ARE YOU! WHY AREN'T YOU ANSWERING THE PHONE!

I slammed my phone onto the coffee table, lit another cigarette, and rubbed my hand through my curly sandy brown hair. I leaned back onto the couch again. I was starting to feel a buzz from the two shots I had taken.

Another hour had gone by without hearing from my husband. Two more shots, and a couple more cigarettes later, I heard him pull into the driveway. I stood up and almost fell over from the dizzy feeling that had rushed over my body. I staggered to the door and opened it right as he was walking up.

"Hey baby." he said to me.

I was standing in the doorway with my silk robe on, arms folded, and bouncing my leg.

"Don't hey baby me." I slurred and rolling my neck.

"What's wrong with you?" he chuckled. My husband leaned down and kissed me.

"What's funny? Where have you been?" I asked.

Laron lightly pushed me into the house. After he closed the door he said, "Have you been drinking?"

"Yes." I said with my eyebrows raised.

"You've been smoking too. Bae, I thought you quit?"

"I've been calling you."

"I know. I accidentally put my phone on silent."

"So, why didn't you call me on your way home?"

"Because the battery was dying bae see."

He showed me his phone. There was only one percent phone battery left. I swayed a little. I was feeling too tipsy.

"I forgot my car charger at home bae."

He walked into the kitchen and picked the charger up off the kitchen table. I don't know how I missed that.

"Why are you tripping? You know me better than that."

"Because I don't like this. At all."

"You don't like what?"

"You and this girl! I know that I said that I was cool with it, but I am not! You're spending all this time with her was not a part of the plan!"

"Alright bae."

"I don't want to do this anymore!"

"Alright bae. I didn't know that it was bothering you like that. Com'ere."

He pulled me to him and kissed me.

"Stop it bae. In here drinking and smoking cigarettes. It's not that serious. You know I love you and only you."

He cupped my ass and then he said, "Go in the room so I can give you this D."

I smiled and headed to the room. I took off my robe and laid down naked. He came in there a few minutes later after he took a shower. He told me to turn over onto my stomach. He started giving me a back massage and then he started massaging my butt. He knows that I love when he does that. It is one of the best feelings in the world. He rubbed me for a little while and then when he saw that I was relaxed, he slowly laid on top of me. He whispered in my ear that he loved me. I told him that I loved him too. He began kissing my neck and shoulders and then I arched my back for him. He grinded into me slow while continuing to massage my butt. The feeling made me get my O quick. He knows exactly what to do to get me there.

"Mmm I love you." I moaned as I began to shake and shiver from the orgasm he gave me.

"I love you too baby." he whispered as he grinded deep into my wetness. He pulled out and flipped me over, so he could be on top. He started tongue kissing me as he put one of my legs on his shoulder. He pounded a little harder while staring into my eyes.

"You like that?" he asked.

"Mmm yes, I doooo." I moaned. He wrapped his lips around one of my nipples and sucked gently while he continued to deep stroke my box. I felt another orgasm, so I wrapped my arms around him and lightly scratch his back.

"Yes, right there, baby. Don't stop." I whispered. He stuck his tongue out and we flicked tongues and then I sucked on his. I stopped and shouted, "Oh yes!"

My walls clinched, and my ocean flooded his manhood and the bed. After he felt me bust, he told me that he was about to cum too. He beat my box a few more times and then he pulled out and spilled his sticky liquid onto my stomach. He kissed me, stood up, and I followed him to the bathroom. He turned on the water to fill the tub as I wiped his man juices from my stomach. After the tub filled, we got in, and bathed together, and then we got out, changed the sheets on the bed, cuddled and pillowed talked until sleep found us.

Chapter 14

Riley

Riley pulled up to her place and found street parking in front of the duplex. She saw Jamir sitting on her porch. Riley got out of her car and used her key ring to pop her trunk. She pulled a few shopping bags out of her trunk, closed it and walked up to the porch.

"What are you doing here?" Riley asked Jamir as she walked up the stairs.

"I wanted to see you." Jamir said. He stood up and walked over to her.

"You couldn't have called? I called you yesterday and you never called me back."

"I am sorry. I was on a flight yesterday. Plus, I wanted to surprise you."

"You were on a flight all night?"

"I was tired. Do we have to talk about this? I miss you. Com'ere." He wrapped his arm around Riley's waist and pulled her to him. He kissed her on the lips.

She blushed and said, "I miss you too."

"Can I come in?" he asked.

"Yes." she said.

Riley used her key to unlock her door and then Jamir followed her up the stairs. Once they were inside of her place, Jamir took his jacket off and hung it on the back of one of Riley's dining room chairs. Jamir took his shoes off, set them by the door, and then he walked over to her couch and sat down. Riley took her shopping bags into her bedroom and put them on her bed. She walked back into the living room. Jamir grabbed her arm as she was walking past the couch and pulled her to him.

Riley started laughing. "What?" she asked when she landed in his lap.

"You looking good, where are you coming from?"

"The Mall of America."

"With who?"

"My sister."

"You sure you weren't on a date?"

"Be quiet Jamir. You know I wasn't on a date." she said. Jamir leaned down and kissed her. Riley returned his kiss and gave him some tongue. He started rubbing her breasts and then he reached down into her pants and rubbed her peach.

"Mmm you wet as hell." Jamir said. He took his hand out of Riley's pants.

"I want you." Riley said.

"Take that off so I can give it to you." Jamir said.

Riley didn't hesitate. She started taking her pants off and unbuttoning her shirt. Riley was taking too long to undress, so Jamir started to kiss her before she could get the shirt all the way off. He laid her on the couch, pulled her panties to the side, and put his manhood inside of her. He sucked on her neck. Riley moaned loudly and wrapped her legs around his waist.

"How bad you want this dick?" Jamir asked.

"I want it bad." Riley responded.

"Oh yea?" Jamir asked as he started pounding harder into her.

"Uhh, yes baby, fuck me." Riley said as she bounced back.

Jamir smiled. He loved how Riley was taking it. He had taught her well. Jamir took both her legs from around him and spread them apart.

"Fuck you like that?"

"Um hum. Like that." she whispered as he deep stroked her wet center. Riley was looking right into his eyes, and Jamir was staring into hers too. He tried to unbutton the rest of her shirt with one of his hands, but he got frustrated and just ripped the shirt open. All the buttons popped off and fell onto the couch and on the floor.

"Damn baby." Riley moaned.

"Don't worry about it. I'll buy you another one." He whispered into her ear. Jamir sucked on her ear lobe, put his tongue into her ear, and then he kissed Riley down her neck and chest until he reached her breasts. Jamir put each one into his mouth, sucked on them, and then he flicked his tongue on her nipples. Jamir was hitting her G spot at the same time. She started moaning louder.

"Ah yes baby fuck this pussy!" Riley moaned.

"I'm on your spot, right?"

"Yea baby stay right there!"

"Um hum. That's it. Get it." he whispered. Jamir knew he had her right where he wanted her. On the brink of an orgasm. He kept his stroke steady and strong. He knew that she was there when he felt her dig her nails into his back. He bit his bottom lip and watched her facial expressions go through changes.

"Ahhh Jamir! I'm about to cum!" she cried out. Riley's eyes rolled into the back of her head as she reached her peak. Her nose wrinkled, and her eyebrows frowned as her orgasm made her body freeze. Riley was ready to tap out after that orgasm. She told Jamir that she couldn't take anymore.

"Nah I'm about to give you another one." Jamir whispered, and then he did exactly what he said three more times.

***

Jamir woke Riley up at about midnight to tell her that he had to go. Riley was so drained that she didn't have the energy to ask Jamir to stay. She slowly slid out of bed and walked with him to the door. Riley was scratching her scalp and yawing as they were walking down the stairs. She wished that he would stay over more instead of leaving in the middle of the night.

"Bye babe. I'm going to call you later, ok?"

"Yes." she said before yawning again.

Jamir chuckled a little and said, "Go back to bed sleepy head."

He kissed her and walked out of the door. Riley closed and locked the heavy wooden door and dragged herself back up the stairs, and climbed back into her bed. Riley pulled her cover over her head and went back to sleep.

***

She woke up in the morning to a text message from Jamir.

I enjoyed you yesterday beautiful.

Riley smiled and got out of bed. She took a shower, got dressed, and left her place to meet Raelyn at the gym. Fall leaves covering the sidewalks reminded Riley that her least favorite season was around the corner. It was that time of year to start preparing for winter. She made a mental note to take her car to Jamir's uncle's shop to get a tune up. Riley turned up a Drake song that was playing on KMOJ radio station. She started snapping her fingers to it as she was driving down Highway 394. She took the ramp to transition onto Highway 100 and then she exited on Cedar Lake Road. Riley pulled into the gym's parking lot a few minutes later. She parked in an empty parking spot. Riley was early as usual which meant Raelyn was either going to be on time or late. She picked up her phone and called Jamir. He didn't answer, so Riley set her phone on the middle console and pulled down the visor mirror to look at herself. She got a text message notification. Riley picked her phone up and swiped the screen to unlock it. She opened the text message from Jamir. She hated when he would text her back after she called him.

9:10 am

Sup babe?

Riley text messaged back.

9:11 am

I just called you.

He responded.

9:12 am

I know. Are you ok?

She responded.

9:13 am

Yes. I am at the gym. Are you coming over later?

Riley saw Raelyn pull into the parking spot next to her. Raelyn waved when she pulled up. She was on time. Riley looked at her phone again, but Jamir hadn't text back yet. She turned her car off and took the keys out of the ignition. She grabbed her purse and got out of the car.

"Yo!" Raelyn said when she got out of her car.

"Yo!" Riley said back. She walked over and gave Raelyn a hug and then she said, "I see you're on time today."

"Um hum. What's wrong with you?" she asked. Raelyn can always sense when something is wrong with Riley even if she tries to hide it. It is the twin bond they have.

"What? Nothing." she said.

"It's Jamir, isn't it? What did he do now?" Raelyn asked as they walked towards the gym.

"No, well, I called him this morning and he text me back. I hate when he does that." Riley said.

The ladies walked over to the treadmill machines once they were inside. They hung their sweat towels over the top of the machine. They started pressing the buttons on the machine to get their settings where they wanted them and then they started their machines and began walking.

"What did he say was the reason for not answering the phone?" Raelyn asked.

"He didn't. He just asked me what I was up to."

"I mean I don't know. Maybe he is busy sister."

"I know he is busy with work sometimes, but this seems to be a regular thing for him and I am like why is it so hard to return a call?"

"Maybe he's not a phone person. Let me stop with the B.S. Do you think that he is messing with someone else?"

"I thought that too, but it couldn't be, as much as we have sex."

"That doesn't mean anything." Raelyn said.

Riley knew that her sister was right. Riley was just in denial. She didn't want to believe that there was someone else. Riley wanted to believe that she was the only woman in his life and they were going to live happily ever after.

Riley replied, "He works a lot but when he is not at work he is with me."

"I mean have you asked him where you guys are at in the relationship?"

"Yea and he is always telling me to chill out, and let things flow naturally."

"Is he telling you that he loves you yet?"

"No. He says that he cares about me."

"Do you love him?"

"I do, and I want us to be official."

"I hear you sister, but you got to be careful with that because I don't want to see you hurt again."

"I know."

Both the women sped up their treadmill speeds and began running. Riley put her ear buds into her ears and set her phone to Pandora music station. Raelyn did the same. Riley was trapped in her thoughts about Jamir and then her text message notification sounded breaking her thoughts. She picked up her phone to check the message. It was from Jamir. He was responding to her text message thirty minutes later.

10:43 am

Yea. I'll hit you later.

Chapter 15

Raelyn

I was back to hanging out with Laron again. I never agreed to meet his wife, in fact, he hadn't brought her up since the night at the restaurant. I liked Laron a lot, so I continued to see him knowing that he had a wife. I gave meeting his wife some thought, but I still wasn't sure that it was something that I wanted to do. I enjoyed spending time with him. When I told Riley that I was still seeing him, she was shocked.

"Are you, serious sister?"

"Yes."

"Why would you do that knowing that he has a wife?"

"Because I like him, and he told me that she is cool with it."

"What woman is cool with her man dating another woman?"

"That is what I said, but he assured me that it was ok. They want me to be involved with them."

"What!? So, they are on some freaky type stuff?"

"No, not just sex. They want to date me."

"You're really going to do it?"

"I don't know. I've been thinking about it."

"How are you going to go from dating no men, to dating a man and his woman, Rae? I mean come on, be for real. Something is wrong with that situation. I wouldn't trust it."

"I don't know. I guess I kind of want to explore and try new things."

I thought about that conversation while walking with Laron around the lake. We found a spot in the grass to sit down to rest before going back to our cars. We sat in the grass looking out at the lake water enjoying the weather. We wanted to get outside and take advantage of one of the last few warm days before winter. There were a lot of people out there who must have had the same agenda. There were people biking, skating, running, pushing strollers, and walking dogs. Some people were sitting at the playground watching their kids play.

I looked down at the ground and picked up one of the red leaves that had fallen from the trees around us. I twirled it in my fingers a couple of times examining it and admiring how pretty it was. I looked back out at the lake. I loved how the reflection of the sun bounced off the water. It made the murky green water look extremely pretty.

"What are you thinking about?" Laron asked.

"Nothing. What are you thinking about?" I asked.

"Just thinking about how I am enjoying this time with you." he said.

"I'm enjoying it too." I said. I picked up a rock and threw it at the water.

"Do you know how to skip a rock?" he asked.

"I used to, but I haven't done it in so long." I said.

"I want to see." he said. I laughed and picked up a rock and tossed it at the lake. I flicked my wrist to make it skip. The rock bounced off the water once and went in. Laron started laughing and clapping.

"Look at you!" he said.

"I know." I laughed. "My twin and I were kind of tom boys when we were kids." I said. Laron picked up a small rock and threw it at the lake, but it didn't skip. I started laughing.

"You're better than me." he said while laughing.

Laron pulled me to him and I laid my head on his shoulder. He kissed me, and I felt butterflies in my stomach. I was falling in love with him, but I wasn't trying to. It was happening naturally. I wasn't sure what I was getting myself into, but it felt good.

"I'm falling in love with you." Laron said.

"Are you?" I asked.

"Yes. I think that you're falling in love with me too." he said.

I continued to look out at the lake in silence for a moment. I didn't want to agree or disagree. I wasn't ready to give in to what I was feeling for him because of the situation.

After a moment of silence, he said, "You don't have to say anything because I already know, and baby this is so perfect. It feels right."

"I have to admit, I feel comfortable with you."

"I know." There was a moment of silence between us again, and then he asked, "So are you ready to meet my wife?"

It was like everything paused. Like that scene in the movie when someone says something shocking and the music stops. The mention of his wife paused our moment and killed our vibe. I hesitated before I spoke. I felt like a cat that had a ball in my throat. Something about him bringing her up made me nervous.

"Um, I don't know."

"It's been a few weeks since we last spoke about it. I think that it is time." he said.

"I like spending time with you, but I am not sure if meeting your wife is something that I want to do yet." I said.

"What's making you so afraid of trying something new?"

"I don't know. It's just. I 've never been in this kind of situation before."

"I understand that, but trust me babe there's nothing to be afraid of. She knows how I feel about you and she wants to meet you."

I sat up and looked down at the grass and then I looked up at the lake. At that moment, I decided to just do it.

"Ok."

"Really?"

"Yes."

The corners of his mouth curled up into a smile. "Come here." he said as he pulled me to him. He hugged me and kissed me.

"I love you. I promise babe that you two will love each other too."

"Alright. We should get something to eat after this. I am starved."

"I know a good place. Let's go."

He stood up and reached out his hand to help me stand up. I stood up and used my hand to brush leaves and grass off my butt. We walked to our cars, and then I followed him in my car to a restaurant that had seating on the roof. It was the perfect day for outdoor dining.

Chapter 16

Paris

I was making my way through my house cleaning and straightening. Making sure that everything was prepared to meet Raelyn for the first time. My husband invited her over for dinner. I felt mixed emotions about it when he told me that he was going to. I wanted to meet the girl that he had been chasing, but another part of me didn't feel ready. Although I was uneasy, I agreed to it and helped him plan for it.

My husband and I cooked the food together and then he stepped out for a minute to pick up a couple bottles of champagne. I opened the stove to check on the food. I closed the oven and turned the temperature down low enough to keep the food warm without over cooking it. I was nervous. I guess because I was about to meet the other woman. I needed to calm down, so I stepped out the back door onto our porch. The night air was chilly. I shivered a little and rubbed my arms. I pulled my grill lighter out of my apron and lit a cigarette. I took a puff and blew the smoke into the air. I hadn't smoked cigarette in a month, but I needed one to calm my nerves.

"I can't believe that I am doing this." I said.

I took another puff and blew the smoke in the air. I rubbed my hands through my sandy brown hair. I had just straightened it that morning. I tapped my foot a couple times on the wood porch. I put the cigarette out in the ashtray I brought out there and threw the butt in the outside trash can. I walked back into the house, washed my hands, washed out the ashtray, and put it back into my hiding space for it. I left the kitchen and walked upstairs to our master bathroom. A few minutes after I got into the shower, I heard my husband walk into the house.

"Baby!" he called out.

"Yes!" I said loudly from the shower.

I heard him walking up the stairs, and then he walked into the bathroom and asked, "Are you about to get dressed?"

I peeked my head out of the shower curtain and said, "Yes."

"Ok. What are you wearing?"

"The jumpsuit that is laying on the bed."

"I love you." he said and then he walked up to me and gave me a kiss.

"I love you too." I said.

He walked out of the bathroom. I finished my shower, got out, and rubbed my favorite Victoria Secrets lotion onto my body. I brushed my teeth and put on a pair of black, lace, thong panties, but no bra. My jumpsuit had thin spaghetti straps that would not allow me to wear a bra. I walked into the bedroom and picked up my satin, black, one-piece, pant suit. I slipped it on and zipped up the back. The spaghetti straps showed off my back and the butterfly tattoo on my shoulder. I brushed my hair and put a side part in it, applied make-up, put on my jewelry, and headed back downstairs. Laron was already dressed and waiting for me.

"You look stunning baby." Laron said when I walked into the living room. He opened his arms for a hug. I walked into his arms and gave him kiss. I wiped my cherry red lipstick from his lips. He lifted one of my arms, so I could spin around in a circle.

"Thank you." I said.

"Wow. You gonna get the business tonight." he said. I blushed and walked away. He smacked me on the butt as I was walking away, so I switched harder for him.

"Um hum. You gonna get it." he called after me.

I walked into the kitchen and turned the stove off. I used an oven mitten to pull the hot pot of food out of the oven and put it on the stove. I started to set the table. I made sure I put her at the head of the table, so she could sit in between us. I didn't want her to sit across from us and make it feel like an interview, although it really was. I also didn't want to sit across from her and look straight into her eyes every time I looked up. After I finished setting the table, I heard the doorbell ring. I took a deep breath, walked into the living room, and stood next to my husband. I felt my heart beating extremely fast. Laron opened the door and she walked in. Laron hugged her and welcomed her and then he introduced us.

"This is my wife Paris. Paris this is Raelyn."

"Nice to meet you." Raelyn said. She extended her hand to shake mine.

I shook her hand and said, "Nice to meet you as well."

I surveyed her beautiful brown skin and her flawless hair. She had these long, gorgeous, jet-black, tresses parted down the middle with loose curls on the ends. I wanted to ask her where she got her hair done, but I didn't want to be too forward or come off rude.

"Welcome to our home." Laron said.

"Can I take your jacket?" I asked.

"Sure." Raelyn said. She removed her leather jacket and handed it to me. That's when I noticed how fit her body was. She was wearing a sweater dress and a pair of ankle boots.

"You're beautiful by the way." she said.

I said, "Thanks, you are too. I like your dress."

"Thank you. I like your jumpsuit." she said.

"Thanks. I will be right back." I walked away with her jacket in hand. Laron walked with her over to the couch. My heart was still racing. I inhaled and exhaled a few times while hanging her jacket in the closet. I wished that I could go outside and smoke a cigarette, but there was no way that I was standing around this beautiful girl smelling like cigarette smoke and give her a reason to be looking at me sideways. I walked back into the living room. Laron and Raelyn were engaged in some small talk.

"Hey baby." he said when he saw me. "I was just telling Raelyn that you're a model."

"Yes, I am." I smiled.

"That's amazing. I have a friend who models." she said.

"What's her name? I might know her."

"Taji Sarii"

"Hmmm. Sounds familiar." I said.

"She is a fairly new model."

"Was that your tall, dark skinned, friend that was at the club?" My husband asked.

"Yes."

"She is gorgeous. I would love to do some photos of her for practice. You should hook it up."

"I will."

"Are you two, ready to eat?" I asked

"Yea." Raelyn said.

My husband and Raelyn stood up and followed me to the dining room table. Laron wrapped his arm around hers as he escorted her through our house to the table.

"Your house is beautiful." Raelyn said as Laron helped her sit down. He walked over and pulled out my chair for me to sit down.

"Thank you." I responded as I was sitting down.

My husband took both of our plates to the kitchen leaving both of us sitting at the table in awkward silence. I decided to break the silence and I said, "Laron told me that you are a bartender."

"Yes." Raelyn replied.

"How long have you been bartending?"

"A couple of years." she said.

"How do you like it?"

"I like the freedom and the money."

"That's nice."

She asked, "How long have you been modeling?"

"Like twenty years."

"Wow." she said.

"I know. I am considered a veteran now. My mom got me into it when I was a kid. I was signed to a modeling agency when I was five years old. I used to do Gap Kids and Old Navy advertisements. I started doing runway stuff once I became a teenager. I still do some runway, but I do mostly print modeling for various magazines and catalogs now. I've traveled all over the world and then I met this knuckle-head and settled here in Minnesota.

"Yea I couldn't have my baby across the map. I needed her right here with me." Laron said when he walked back into the dining room. He set my plate in front of me and then kissed me. He set her plate in front of her and then went back into the kitchen to make his plate.

Raelyn asked, "Where are you from?"

"California." I said. Laron sat down with his plate.

"How did you two, meet?" Raelyn asked. I had a mouth full of food, so I looked up at Laron. He smiled at me and laughed.

"Ok I will tell the story." He took his napkin and wiped his mouth.

"We met on a photoshoot for a magazine. It was her and three other girls. She had all this attitude."

"I did not." I laughed.

"Yes, you did." Laron said.

"I guess she thought she was the shit because she was a vet. I didn't like her attitude, but I thought she was gorgeous. I decided to try to make her laugh during the photo shoot and it worked. She wanted your boy after that."

"Shut up." I said. Raelyn laughed.

I said, "I thought he was cute, so we exchanged numbers after the shoot and here we are."

After Raelyn finished laughing at us, she took a bite of her food.

"Well I already know how you two met, so tell me why you like my husband?" I asked.

I admit the question had a little shade underneath it, but I delivered it with a smile. She looked at me as she washed down her bite of her food with some champagne. I couldn't tell if she picked up on the shade or not.

Raelyn smiled and said, "Well I find him to be very attractive and charismatic. I'm sure the same reasons that you fell in love with him when you met on that photoshoot."

I smiled and swallowed down some more champagne.

Laron said, "Thank you. I find you very attractive too." He touched her hand. The slight display of affection sent chills through me, but I stayed calm.

"Did I tell you that Raelyn showed me how to skip a rock the other day at the lake? I didn't know that she had it in her." he said and laughed. Raelyn laughed with him and said, "I told you that I was a tomboy growing up."

"Yea but I didn't believe you." he said and then they laughed with each other.

I watched them talk for a while as I drank my champagne. Part of me was getting pissed because they were getting along too well. *I hope this chick does not think that she is gonna come along and steal my husband with her cute body and smile.* I thought. I gave them a fake smile and took a gulp of my drink. Laron noticed that I was silent and asked, "Are you still interested in going to Vegas? Paris and I would love for you to come."

No, I wouldn't. I thought. "Yea, we would." I said. It was a feigned attempt at being excited about it.

"Um, sure." Raelyn said looking at the both of us.

"Cool." Laron said. He leaned over and kissed her on the cheek. My inner self wanted to jump over the table and rip his lips off her face, but I ignored the feeling. I focused on keeping my breathing steady. I knew right then that I wasn't ready for it. I was ok with it just being sexual, but this is turning into something else. Raelyn smiled at him bashfully. The look in her eyes told me that she was really feeling my husband. It was starting to feel like Raelyn was in love with my husband and I didn't like that. I could feel my heart beating rapidly.

"Do you like cheesecake?" he asked her.

"I love cheesecake." she smiled.

"Well I guess we are ready for desert then. I'll take your plates. We can take desert to the living room. Her and

I stood after he took our plates. She followed me to the living room. Laron brought us each a small plate with a small slice of cheesecake on it and fresh glasses of champagne. He turned on our large flat screen TV and sat down in between us. A reality show came on the screen.

"Do you watch this show?" I asked Raelyn.

"Yes, I love it. The Hollywood cast is my favorite."

"Mine too, I like the New York and Atlanta cast too."

"Me too. It's my guilty pleasure."

My husband said, "I only watch this when Paris makes me. I have to admit that it is entertaining sometimes."

I looked at Raelyn and asked, "How old are you? If you don't mind me asking."

"I don't mind. I'm twenty-six."

"No kids?"

"No not yet. How old are you?"

"Thirty-one." I said

"Yea. Just one-month shy of being a cougar." Laron said.

"Shut up." I said and punched him.

He laughed and said, "My birthday is a month after hers, but we are the same age."

"Oh ok."

"So how do you feel about us being older than you?"

"It's not like your fifty." she said.

"My husband and I laughed and then I took a sip of my drink.

"I like your sense of humor." I said.

"Thank you. Well, I enjoyed this wonderful evening with you two. Thanks for the wonderful dinner and desert, but I have got to get going." Raelyn said. She sat her half-eaten cheesecake on the table next to her half glass of champagne and stood up.

"You're welcome. I will go and get your jacket." I said.

I walked out of the living room. When I came back with her jacket in hand, her and my husband were waiting and talking by the door. I handed her the jacket. As she put it on she said, "It was nice to meet you."

"You as well." I said. I shook her hand.

Laron hugged her and said, "Thank you for coming. He opened the door for her and watched her until she got into her car. He closed and locked the door. I was leaning on the back of the couch with my arms folded.

"So, that's her huh?" I asked.

"Yup."

"What's so special about her?" I asked with my face screwed.

"Come on now. She is pretty, and she is sweet."

"Whatever." I rolled my eyes.

"I know that you're not jealous?" he asked. I rolled my eyes again.

He chuckled. "You better stop it." He stood in front of me and wrapped his arms around my waist. "You know damn well, you have nothing to be worried about. There ain't no woman better than you. You hear me?" he said.

I stared into his light brown eyes. "Um hum."

"Um hum what?'

"Ok I hear you."

"Give me a kiss." he said. I put my lips on his and he gave me a passionate tongue kiss. His hand rubbed one of my breasts and then my lower lips. I felt my kitty purr when I felt his soft touch.

"Grab that bottle of champagne and meet me in the bedroom." he said lustfully. I gave him a devilish grin. I turned and put my soft ass on his dick print. He was rock hard, and it was showing through his pants. I leaned over the couch and reached for the bottle on the table. I knew that I couldn't reach it. I just did it to entice him even more.

"Keep playing and you're gonna get this D right here."

"Maybe I want it right here."

"Is that how you feel?"

"Yes."

He didn't say another word. He unzipped my jumpsuit in the back. He pushed the straps off my shoulders and watched it fall to the floor. He pulled my panties down. I stepped out of them and my jumpsuit, but I kept my heels on

"Stay just like that." he said.

I stayed bent over the couch while my husband took his clothes off. He went to the kitchen and came back with a bottle of chocolate syrup. He poured a little down the crack of my ass. He bent down and started licking the syrup off my ass, and then he pulled my cheeks apart and licked all the syrup that had gone inside. I moaned and gripped the decorative couch pillows. He moaned as he ate my booty like groceries. Judging by the slurping noises he was making. It sounded like the best sweet treat he had ever eaten. He poured some more chocolate on my ass and licked it off and then he began sucking the chocolate that had drizzled down to my peach. He paid special attention to my pearl. I moaned his name and squeezed the couch pillows some more when I felt him wrap his soft lips around my clit. He slurped and sucked on my clit until I screamed out his name.

"Ah! Laron!" I froze for a few seconds and then I released my juices onto his soft lips.

"Mmmm." he said when he tasted my sweet nectar. He stood up and smacked me on my sticky ass. He eased himself inside me from behind and then whispered how much he loved my juice box in my ear.

"I love this pussy baby." My husband whispered.

"I love this dick." I moaned.

He reached down and rubbed my clit while grinding me from the back, I bounced my soft ass on his manhood. My husband loves when I make my booty clap while he is hitting it from behind.

"You know I like that. Give me that pussy." My husband whispered.

He then placed his hands on my sticky ass and pounded into me just the way I like it. I held on to the back of couch as I felt my husband fill me up with all his love. He sucked on my shoulder and my neck, and then I leaned my head back, so he could kiss my lips. I returned his feverish kiss with one of my own. Tasting and sucking the mixture of chocolate sauce and my nectar off his soft pink lips. He held onto my sticky ass and pounded into me continuously until my moans turned to yelps that it was good. I started begging him not to stop. The sound of my voice echoed through the house telling my husband that I was cuming. He groaned and grunted and then I screeched, "Ah! Yes!"

My juices poured onto him as my body shook and he told me to get mine, and then he pulled out and stepped back. I felt my juices dripping down my leg. He smiled walked over to the coffee table, picked up the bottle of champagne, and told me "Come on."

I knew that meant he wasn't ready to cum yet. He wanted to put it down some more. I gathered myself and our clothes and followed him upstairs to our bedroom where we continued our love making. That night, we were making love for hours. That night, our love making lasted all night. That night, I loved every moment of making love to my husband, and it was the last night that I had him all to myself.

Chapter 17

Raelyn

"Your wife doesn't like me." I said.

I put my hands on my hips and rocked back and forth a little. I had just finished a run around Loring Park. I was still trying to catch my breath. Winter season was nearing, and I was trying to enjoy a few more runs around the park before it would be too cold to be outside running. I refuse to even try to run outside in the winter. I am too afraid of slipping and falling on a patch of ice. I would have run a little longer that day, but Laron wanted to stop by and talk to me before he headed home to his wife. He was standing outside of his car with his back leaning up against the driver's side door when I jogged up. He had on a brown leather jacket and his sandy brown dreads were hanging lose around his shoulders.

Laron asked, "Why would you say that?"

"Because I can tell. Are you sure that she is ok with doing this?" I asked.

"She is fine. Trust me. She likes you."

"Well her energy says something different. She was smiling, but she was covering her true feelings." I said and then I lifted one of my feet. I pulled it backwards to stretch my thigh muscles. I did the same to my other foot and thigh.

Laron said, "Nah she was just nervous like you were. It was both of your first-time meeting each other, so it was bound to be awkward babe. Don't trip. She's with it. She will open up just give her some time."

"I don't know." I said.

"Nah babe, don't back out now. Spend some more time with us and you will feel better. I promise."

I twisted my lips in the air and he laughed. He pulled me to him and gave me a hug.

"I love you." he said.

"I love you too." I replied.

"I got to get going, but I will call you later."

I said, "Alright." I waited for him to get in his car, waved at him, and then I turned and walked into my apartment building.

***

"You told me that yesterday." Riley said into her phone.

We were at the Mall of America in a clothing store shopping for some winter clothes. Snow had finally fallen, and I wanted to get a new pair of Ugg boots, a couple of sweaters, and maybe a couple pair of jeans if I could find the right fit. I was listening to Riley while still looking through a rack of clothes.

"Don't say that if you're not going to do it." Riley said. She was silent for a moment and then she said "Aight." She hung up and put her phone into her coat pocket.

"That must have been Jamir." I said.

"Yes, it was." she said irritably.

"What's up with that?" I said as I followed her to the next rack of clothes. We began to search through the items.

"He starts coming over a lot and showing up when he says he is going to and then he just stops. I don't know what his problem is."

"Why do you put up with it sis?" I asked.

"I don't know. Every time I say I'm done, I let him back in. He was supposed to come over yesterday, but he didn't show up. He text messaged me an hour after he was supposed to be there to tell me that he wasn't going to make it. He just called to tell me that he will be over tonight."

"Have you ever been to his house?"

"Yea. He's living with his mom right now until he gets his own place. I met her, and she was really nice."

"That's cute."

Riley said, "I know. She seems like she likes me."

We walked with our pile of clothes through the store towards the dressing rooms.

I said, "I have something to tell you."

"What?" she asked nonchalantly. The mess with Jamir was still bothering her. I could see it in her body language.

"I met her."

"Who?"

"His wife."

"Shut up!" she exclaimed. Her body language changed when I said that. She stopped walking and turned to me. I nodded my head up and down.

"What happened?" she asked.

"Nothing happened. They invited me over for dinner and that was it."

"Oh, my God sister. What was she like? What did she look like?"

"Well, she is tall and extremely gorgeous. Her skin complexion is like Beyoncé's. She has pretty, light brown eyes just like Laron. I wanted to ask her if she is mixed, but I didn't want to be rude. She doesn't have one ounce of body fat on her. She told me that she is a model and has been modeling for like twenty years."

"Wow."

"I know. They look good together, but I don't think that she likes me."

"Why do you say that?"

"She was nice and polite, but I felt like she was hating, and masking it with a smile."

"Mmm." Riley said and then we walked into the dressing rooms. "Maybe she isn't as cool with the situation as he makes it seem."

"I feel the same sister. I asked him, and he said that she was just nervous."

We tried on a few items and walked out of the dressing rooms to show each other what we liked and what we didn't like. It all came down to, we didn't like anything, so we gave all the items to the fitting room attendant and headed out of the store.

"Are you going to go through with it?"

"I don't know." I said.

We walked through the enormous mall, past the indoor amusement park, towards the indoor aquarium, and up the escalator, to the second floor. We continued to walk to the left, away from the middle rotunda, past a few shoe stores, towards the other side of the mall where Lego Land is located.

"On another note, their house is amazing. Fire place, elegant décor, spotless clean, expensive furniture. I was shocked at how nice it was." I said as we walked into the store we were heading to.

"Well what were you expecting a run-down dump?"

I laughed and said, "No, but I wasn't expecting such elegance."

She laughed. "How did he act?"

"He was cool."

"I bet he was. What man wouldn't be around two beautiful women that he is going to have sex with?"

"I guess you have a point." I laughed. We found a few items that we liked and headed towards the dressing rooms.

"I don't know sis. I'm not sold on your situation, but if your happy, I am too."

"I feel that same about your situation." We walked into the dressing room area. The dressing room attendant gave us numbers and walked us in.

Triangles

Chapter 18

Riley

"I see you decided to actually show up." she said to Jamir when he walked in the door of her place.

He stomped his boots on the floor mat to remove snow. Riley hurriedly closed the heavy wooden door to block the strong, icy cold, wind that was blowing in. She locked the door and began walking up the stairs to her place.

"Hush that fuss woman." Jamir said as he followed her up the wooden stairs. He closed door once they were inside and then he took off his boots and placed them on the floor mat by the door. He took his coat off and hung it on her coat hanger.

"I see you've been doing a lot of shopping lately." He said looking at the shopping bags by the door. Riley didn't get around to putting her things away. He called right after she'd made it home from shopping with Raelyn to tell her that he was on the way. Riley had to get into the bath quickly and straighten her place before he got there. She didn't even get the chance to put some clothes on because he was ringing her bell right after she put some moisturizer on her skin.

"Yea. Retail therapy." Riley said as she adjusted her robe and retied it.

He laughed. "Was that directed towards me?"

"Yea."

He laughed again and asked, "Why?"

"Because you're driving me crazy." she said. Riley had her hand on her hip. Jamir wrapped his arms around her waist and pulled her to him.

"Get that frown off you face. You know that you're my bae." he said

Riley stood there with the same expression on her face and her hand still on her hip.

"Um hum." she responded.

"Bae stop." he chuckled. "I'm sorry I couldn't make it yesterday. I got tied up."

Riley exhaled loudly.

"Are you seeing someone else?" she asked.

"No. I don't have time to see anyone else. I barely have time to see you."

"Where is this going?"

"What do you mean?"

"Us. Where are, we going? I told you how I feel about you several times and I'm starting to feel like this isn't going anywhere." Riley removed his arms from around her waist.

"I told you that we are chilling for right now and building, but you're my bae though and you know that."

"How long are we going to be quote unquote building?" Riley used her hands to do the quotation gestures.

Jamir looked her up and down. He wasn't ready for her attitude or her questions.

"What's up with you? Why are you giving me all this attitude?" he asked.

"I'm trying to figure out what's up with you? I want to be with you and I want to know what we are doing?"

"You're tripping right now."

"I'm tripping? Because I want to know what we're doing? Are you telling me that this is going to be like the last time?" she asked.

He scratched his head and said, "I ain't with all this drama."

"Now it's drama?" she asked

"Yea. I'm about to go."

"Fine. Leave then." Riley said. She walked over to her couch, plopped down, crossed her arms over her chest and then crossed her legs. Riley watched him put his boots and coat back on and walk out the door. Jamir slammed the door behind him. Riley listened to his footsteps down the steps and then she heard the heavy wood door slam. She wiped a tear, stood up, walked over to the window and watched him pull off in his car. With her arms still folded, she walked back to her door, down the stairs, and locked the door. Once she got back into her place, she closed and locked her door, grabbed her cell phone from the table, sat down on the couch and called her sister. Raelyn didn't answer, so she sent a text message.

Call me when you can.

Chapter 19

Raelyn

I hung out with Paris and Laron and again. He took us on a movie and dinner date. Paris was still giving me the same energy she had the night we had dinner at their place. She was still smiling and being polite, so I ignored it.

The next weekend they invited me to the theater to see a stage play that was in town. I was going to turn down the offer because of the way I felt about Paris, but I decided to give it one more try and if I wasn't feeling it that time, I was going to back out of the situation.

Laron was a perfect gentleman as usual, and Paris seemed a bit more open with the idea of the three of us. The play was amazing, and I enjoyed myself. As we were walking out of the theater Paris said, "I want to have a real drink. Those drinks in there were weak."

I laughed and said, "Yes they were."

"We should stop in this restaurant before we go home." Paris said.

"You cool with that?" Laron asked me.

"Yea."

"Aight." Laron said.

My legs were freezing as we walked down the street from the theater to the restaurant. It was ten degrees outside and I was wearing a dress and some boots. Paris was wearing the same thing, so I was sure that her legs were cold too. I should have worn jeans, but I was trying to be dressed up for the theater. Paris walked next to me and not next to him which was a change. We sat down at an empty booth. She sat next to me. I started to feel like she was keeping her enemy closer.

"You two look beautiful tonight, but I know that y'all cold in those dresses." Laron said.

We laughed and then Paris said, "Yes we are."

"So, what are we drinking bartender?" Paris asked me.

"Well, what do you like?" I asked.

"You're the professional. Give us your best recommendation." she said.

"You seem like a martini type and he is the Hennessy and coke type."

"Good observation." she said.

"Thank you. Have you ever tried a lemon drop martini? It's my favorite." I said.

"No, but I will tonight." she said.

We ordered our drinks when the waiter made it over to our table.

Paris asked, "Did you enjoy the play?"

I said, "Very much so."

"I saw you over there laughing at some parts." she said.

"I was." I said.

Paris smiled and looked up when the waiter returned with our drinks. She thanked the waiter and took a sip of her lemon drop martini, and then she said, "Mmmm. This is good. You were right. I do like this."

I smiled and took a sip of my drink.

"I see you know your stuff." Paris said.

"I do." I said.

"That's going to be your new favorite drink baby." Laron said.

"It really is babe." Paris said as she took another sip. Laron laughed, and I smiled. He and I caught eye contact from across the table and I felt tingles. She looked at him and then at me. I broke eye contact with him and pulled my cell phone out of my pocket. I got a text message from my sister that said to call her. I made a mental note to make sure I called her after the date. I put my phone back into my handbag. I decided to ask some questions.

"Do you have siblings back in California?" I asked Paris.

Paris replied, "Yes. I have an older brother and sister."

"Do you ever go home to visit your family?"

"All the time. Do you have siblings?" she asked.

"Yes, I have a twin sister and an older brother."

"You have a twin?"

"Yes. I thought you knew?" I laughed.

"You didn't tell me she had a twin." Paris said to Laron.

"I thought you knew babe. I showed you her social media profile."

"I looked but I didn't see any pics of you and your twin."

"Oh, yea because most of my profile pics are just of me. The pics of me and her are in my timeline photos."

Paris said, "Oh ok. Well, I wasn't digging that hard. I wasn't trying to be a creeper you know. I was just trying to see what you looked like."

I laughed. Seemed like the liquor was loosening her up a little. We chatted about family for a little while longer and then I excused myself to the bathroom.

"Excuse me. I am going to go to the ladies' room." I said.

"Ok." Laron said.

"I'll come with you." Paris said. She slid out of the booth first and then I slid out. She stopped to give Laron a kiss while I was adjusting my dress. We chatted about not falling in our heels on the way to the restroom. After we used the bathroom, we stood at the mirror to refresh our make-up.

Paris asked, "How does it feel to be a twin?"

"Sometimes it feels like I'm fighting for my own identity, but I love it. I truly have a best friend for life.

"That's really special."

"Thanks"

"You know. You seem really cool." she said.

I looked at Paris through the mirror and said, "Are you sure? Because I was under the impression that you didn't like me."

"Did I come off like that?" she asked.

"Um hum." I said while applying more lipstick.

"It wasn't like that. I was just feeling a little uncomfortable." Paris said looking back at me through our reflections in the mirror.

"Why?" I asked.

She turned to face me and said, "Woman to woman. I just hoping that you didn't plan to come and try to steal my husband."

"Steal your husband? Y'all invited me in." I chuckled.

Her mentioning her worries about her husband being taken made me wonder if she knew that her husband told me that he loved me several times, and I wondered if she knew that he had given me the best head ever a couple times. I kept it to myself. It wasn't my business to tell. He said they were open with each other about everything, so she had to know.

Paris said, "I know, but my husband orchestrated the whole thing and he was spending a lot of time with you,

I was hoping that we were all on the same page you know?"

"I understand, and I don't want to steal anyone. This is new for me too."

"Seems like you really like my husband."

"I do." I said.

"I can tell that he really likes you too." she said.

"Yea we have good chemistry, but I am not trying to steal him. I knew what it was when I made the decision to move forward."

Paris nodded her head and then she asked, "So, are you a lesbian?"

"No, are you?"

"No."

Both of us laughed.

"Like I said, I'm just trying something new." I said.

"Me too girl."

"So, are we cool now?" I asked.

"Yes." Paris smiled at me. I smiled back, and we left the bathroom.

Laron stood up to greet us when we made It back to the table. He kissed her on the lips and then he kissed me on the cheek.

"What happened in the bathroom that made you two come back smiling?"

"Nothing." We said at the same time and then we laughed.

"Uh-huh. Something happened." he laughed.

"Nothing happened baby." Paris said. She stood up and sat next to him. She kissed him again.

"Ok." Jamir said. He looked over at the bar and said, "There goes my boy Jamir. Excuse me ladies. I'll be right back." He stood up and walked over to Jamir who was standing at the bar by himself.

"Do you know him?" she whispered from across the table.

"Yea. He talks to my sister."

"Your twin?"

"Um hum."

"I don't like him."

"Tell your sister to be careful. He is a hoe. I hate when my husband hangs with him." She whispered. We noticed that Laron was walking back over to the table with Jamir, so we cut the conversation.

"Ladies you know Jamir, right?" Laron asked. Both of us nodded and said hello to him.

"Aight my dude. I got to break out. It was good seeing you ladies." Jamir slapped hands with Laron and walked away. I could have sworn I saw some girl meet him at the door, but he turned her around and they left.

"You know that I don't like him." Paris said to Laron.

"I know baby, but that's my boy." Laron said. He walked over to my side of the table and then he looked at Paris and asked, "Do you mind?"

"No." she said.

He sat down next to me. "Are you enjoying yourself?" he asked me.

"Yes."

"Good." he said kissing my cheek afterwards.

"Do you ladies want another round?"

"Sure." I said. Paris nodded her head. Laron signaled for the waitress to come back to our table. He ordered another round of drinks for us.

After the second round of drinks all of us were loose, joking, and laughing. Paris seemed more open and free. I felt more comfortable around the two of them. I was having blast. The two of them together were a riot. There wasn't as much tension as there was the first couple times we hung out.

"Aight, fuck it. I want to see you two kiss." Paris said loosely. I could tell that she was feeling the liquor a little bit.

"Are you sure?" Laron asked.

"Um hum." Paris said after swallowing down the last of her second drink. Laron smiled and then he pulled my chin to him and gave me a passionate kiss with a lot of tongue.

"Dang, you don't kiss me like that babe." she said.

"Yes, I do. Stop it." Laron chuckled.

I laughed and wiped the left-over wetness from my lips. He stood up and sat next to her and kissed her the same way that he kissed me. I knew that I was feeling the liquor because I was a little turned on by it. When they finished kissing, Paris smiled at me. I smiled back and said, "You two make a cute couple."

"Thank you." she said. "I'm not going to lie; you and my husband look good together too."

"You think so?" I asked.

"Um hum." she responded and then she told Laron to order some more drinks.

By time the third drink was finished, Paris was sitting next to me with her hand on my leg. We were giggling and talking about nothing that was important. Halfway through the fourth drink, I was gone and way beyond my limit. Paris was past her drinking limit too. She told me that she thought that I was beautiful and then she kissed me. It was a peck, but it was enough for all of us to know that the boundaries had been crossed.

Laron paid the bill and we headed out. When I stood up, I almost stumbled and Paris caught me. We laughed about it while standing at the door waiting for

Laron to pull up with their car. When he arrived, Paris climbed into the back seat with me. That first kiss at the table opened the door because she came right at me for a second one as soon as she closed the car door, and then suddenly, we couldn't stop kissing each other. It was so steamy in the back seat with her and I that Laron could barely keep his eyes on the road while driving back to their house.

When we made it to their house, Paris held my hand and walked me upstairs to their bedroom and Laron followed us. I was too gone to even care about what I was doing.

"Y'all go ahead I just want to watch for a minute." he said.

Both of us took off out boots and dresses and then we began kissing again. Her lips were softer than Laron's and her kiss was more erotic. I had never kissed a girl in my life and kissing her was better than any kiss that I'd ever had. We tasted each other's tongues while Laron stood behind us watching. She put her soft manicured hand on my breast and rubbed one of my hardened nipples as we kissed, and then I did the same to her. She reached behind me to unhook my bra. Once mine was off, I took off hers.

We stopped to examine each other's bodies. Mine, chocolate brown, and athletic. Hers, peanut butter, slim, and soft. My breasts a little smaller than hers. My areola circles and nipples much darker than her shade of tan.

"You are beautiful." she whispered.

"So are you." I responded.

"She is gorgeous babe." She smiled at Laron.

He said, "I know."

Paris stepped back to me, pressed her hard nipples up against mine and started kissing me again. Laron undressed down to his boxers and then he approached us and joined in the kiss. The three of us tasted each other's tongues and lips and then she watched Laron kiss me for a few seconds before putting one of my breasts in her mouth. I felt like I was floating. I had never been kissed and had my nipples sucked on at the same time.

"Lay down." he whispered to me. After I laid down, he said to Paris, "Taste her."

She did what he asked. Paris crawled onto the bed and put her soft lips on my box ever so gently. She kissed it a few times and then used two fingers to separate my lips.

She wrapped her soft, tan colored lips around my pearl, sucked on it softly, and then she slowly and gently rubbed and flicked her tongue on it.

"Mmmm." I moaned out loud. Her head game was better than her husbands.

"That's right." Laron said when he heard me moaning. He watched for a moment and then he bent down and helped his wife give me oral pleasure. They licked and sucked on me together. I watched them take turns on me and then they began flicking their tongues on my pearl at the same time. I grabbed the sheets and moaned obscenities to the ceiling. Laron let Paris take over and then he stood up and told Paris that she looked sexy as hell.

"That's right. Do it like that. Stay on it." he said.

Laron walked behind her and smacked her ass. She got onto her knees and he pushed his tool inside her from behind. He kept his eyes on her licking me while he deep stroked his wife. She whined a little when he hit the right spot. Laron leaned forward so he could help her taste me again. I felt my O and then I heard her moan that she was about to cum. My back arched when I got mine.

"Ah!" I moaned loudly towards the ceiling.

Nia Rich

"Baby I'm cuming!" she yelled.

My body froze for a few seconds, and hers shook a little. Laron started kissing her as she was feeling the aftershock from her orgasm.

"This is so sexy." Paris whispered to him.

"I know." he whispered back.

Laron pulled out of her, put a condom on, and then he climbed on top of me. He stared into my eyes first before he entered me. This was going to be our first time making love to each other. Although his wife was right there in the room with us, for that moment, it felt like it was just me and him. Laron leaned down to kiss me. He took his time going in. It was like he wanted me to feel every inch of him, or maybe he wanted to feel all of me. I moaned when I felt his thickness slide inside of me. I did not know that he was working with all that. A purring sound escaped from my lips as he grinded his manhood into me in slow circular motion. Once he was all the way in, he stayed deep inside using his tool to search for my G spot. Paris laid on the side of me watching her husband make love to me. She looked just as shocked as I felt that it was all happening.

Laron looked at Paris and said, "Come here baby."

She crawled over to him and kissed him and then she came to me and put one of my breasts into her mouth. He smacked her on the ass and told her to put it on my face. Paris crawled up to my face and placed her peach on my lips. She was facing the wall and holding on to the headboard. She slightly grinded her hips on to my face. I tasted her sweetness. I listened to her sounds. Her moans made me feel like I was doing it right, so I kept at it.

Paris looked down at me and whispered, "Yes, right there."

"Get it baby." he said. Laron knew his wife's sounds and he could tell that she was about to cum.

Paris screamed out, "Ah!"

She creamed on my lips, and then she crawled off me and tasted her essence from my lips. Laron pulled out of me and laid down on his back. He told his wife to get on top of him and he told me to climb onto his face. Paris and I were both riding him, and he was giving us both pleasure at the same time. I looked down at him and watched him eat my peach. He was slurping and licking like it was his last meal. I spread my lips a little wider for him to get to my center. I began grinding my hips and moaning louder. I could hear Paris bouncing on him and moaning louder too. The sounds and the feeling put me in a zone. I grabbed the headboard and started going for mine. Laron smacked my ass. That boosted my adrenaline. I started talking to him and telling him how good it felt and to not stop. I felt Paris tap my ass a couple of times, and then I lost control. My orgasm rocked my body. I screeched a couple of obscenities before rolling off his face onto the bed next to him. I had my eyes closed while trying to get myself back together. I heard Paris moan that another orgasm was coming. I heard her hit a high note, so I opened my eyes and looked at them. They looked sexy making love to each other. Her body was limp from her orgasm, but Laron was gripping her waist and pounding upwards into her. She had her hands on his chest, and he was telling her to tell him that she loved it.

"I love it." Paris said.

Laron made a deep growl like sound and then he busted into her. Paris rolled off him onto the bed on the other side of him. When it was all over, the sun was coming up, and we passed out in the bed together. It was done. I had had my first threesome with Laron and his wife.

To Be Continued………

Contact the Author

Email: **niarichbooks@gmail.com**

Instagram: **@authorniarich**

Facebook: **@authorniar**

Twitter: **authorniarich**

www.ingramcontent.com/pod-product-compliance
Lightning Source LLC
Chambersburg PA
CBHW020407150626
46554CB00012B/409